Poised [illegible]

by Morgan W. Silver

POISED TO QUILL

First edition. July 1, 2020.

ISBN: 9789083038841

Written by Morgan W. Silver

Also by Morgan W. Silver

Maggie's Murder Mysteries
Prelude to Poison
Poised to Quill

Monday Moody
The Chrono Unit

Standalone
The Exciting Life of a Minor Character

Watch for more at www.authormw.com.

I dedicate this novel to Granny.

Chapter 1

Pain shot through my wrists. "Come on, come on," I muttered as I wiggled my hands in the rope. My only hope of escape was to move my hands up and down, though that made the pain worse. Stuff like this seemed easier in films. Perhaps I could let myself fall backwards and the chair would magically break. Then again, I liked this chair.

I started to jump up and down, as if that would help. I was running out of time and sighed with defeat.

"Three, two, one," Christina said. "The bomb went off. You're dead." She stopped the timer on her Samsung and took a sip of her ice tea.

"Not me," I said. "Detective Black." We had moved the kitchen chair into the living room where Christina, my flatmate and friend, had tied me up. "But this is quite the pickle. I need Detective Black to be able to get out. Maybe it's because the rope is too tight."

"Hate to break it to you, Mags, but bad guys don't exactly leave wiggle room when tying someone up. I'm guessing," she added and ran a hand through her cool pixie cut. As a former beautician, she knew how to style herself. She'd even helped me with my makeover a couple of months earlier. My wardrobe and hair were better for it. I had a cute bob, feminine outfits, and nicer makeup. More importantly, I felt more like myself.

Since she'd moved in, she'd also made some nice additions to my decor. There were now seasonal cushions that adorned the sofa, and they matched the blankets that she'd put in a basket next to the TV above the fireplace.

"Which means that I'll need to give Detective Black a knife. And a reason to carry a knife before he actually gets into trouble. I've never written that he carries a knife before, so—" my voice trailed off. "Could you perhaps untie me? I do plan on using my hands today."

"Really? I thought you were going to the Summer Festival in that chair. It looks so good on you."

"Ha-ha," I said dryly while Snowball, my bunny, ran circles around my feet. Her white floppy ears had turned grey, and she'd grown in the last few months. I picked her up as soon as Christina freed me and joined her on the sofa. Snowball sat quietly and occasionally sniffed my yellow dress.

"You do the strangest things for research," Christina muttered.

Detective Black popped up next to me with his dark hair and darker eyes, looking every bit like I imagined him. "Don't tell her about that time you made a man out of pillows, just so you could strangle him from various positions. Or all the times you tried all those pastries, just so you could describe the flavour really well. Supposedly."

When I looked up to glare at him, he was already gone.

"Maggie?" Christina asked. "You okay?"

"Yeah. Fine. Just talking to my imaginary friends." Ever since she'd moved in—after Alistair broke up with her—she'd witnessed me talking to myself and my characters, as well as covering the entire wall of my office in post-its. Some of them even ended up on my face, which I hadn't realised until we sat down for dinner. There were moments I'd practise falling, for research purposes, or try out an attack move on Christina.

Surprisingly, she'd liked all of those moments, and she was easy to live with. She'd also become a good friend and employee. I was lucky she'd accepted the job at The Wicked Bookworm; I had needed her ever since one of my bookshop employees turned out to be a murderer.

The first month after moving in, she'd mentioned Alistair a lot. She was truly heartbroken, and I felt torn. Alistair and I had feelings for each other when we were teens, and they'd resurfaced when he'd returned to Castlefield. He'd neglected to tell me he had a girlfriend, but we decided to stay friends. When he broke it off with her, I wasn't sure what it meant, or if it had anything to do with me. I'd never asked. In fact, both Christina and I had done a good job of avoiding him. We'd seen him in the pub a few times, but he'd leave soon thereafter. And despite the fact that this Cornish village ate gossip for breakfast, nobody had anything to spill about Alistair. He kept his feelings close to his chest and me in the dark.

We hardly spoke about him now, even if I thought about him a lot. He had stuff to figure out, and I was glad that he was working on it. At least, I assumed he was. But the selfish part of me wanted to spend time with him, even as friends. I liked his smile, his smell, his magic tricks. I grinned as I thought about him, then adopted a more neutral expression.

"Will you be okay going to the Summer Festival? It will be busy." *Alistair will be there.*

"I know," she said. "I'd like to go. Ten days of summer festivities sound too cute to pass up. Besides, I can't avoid him forever." She gave me a smile.

"Yeah, I know." Snowball hopped over to Christina, and she stroked her soft ears.

"So, what's today again?" she asked.

"Today we have horseshoe throwing."

"And then tomorrow you have your writer thing?" she asked.

"Yeah, the panel of mystery authors. They'll be here today, so we'll see them, I'm sure." I had invited four fellow mystery authors that my agent had put me in touch with. They were interested in joining the Summer Festival in return for free exposure. We would all read parts of our latest novels and do a signing.

Downstairs the door banged, and someone rushed up the stairs. Before I could register who those footsteps belonged to, Eddie's red mop of hair came into view, followed by his freckled face and flushed cheeks. "Nancy," he wheezed, since, like me, he had the stamina of a comatose walrus.

My mind immediately pictured my aunt Nancy having a heart attack, so I dashed past him and ran down the stairs. The door on the right would lead to the street and was the main entrance to my flat, the door on my left would lead to my bookshop. Since Nancy was in her adjacent shop, it was quicker to go through the left one. I sprinted through my bookshop, gaining the looks of a few customers, as well as of Brian, Eddie's friend and my sometimes-employee. He held up his finger as if he was going to say something.

"Not now, Brian." I darted past the counter and went through the curtain that led to a small space where we stored a few boxes, but it also functioned as the world's tiniest break room. I went through the velvet curtain on the other side and stepped into my aunt's occult store. It smelt of incense, and it was somewhat darker in here than in my own shop.

A small crowd had gathered in the middle of the shop, and with my heart nearly leaping out of my chest, I pushed past Eleanor, the vicar's wife, whose grey bun I recognised from behind. I looked down. Nancy was indeed on the floor. Well, not entirely.

She was sitting on someone who was on the floor, and she had a triumphant gleam in her eyes. Well, one eye, the other was made of glass. Nobody knew how it had happened; the stories she told people became more gruesome each time. Yesterday I heard her tell an American tourist that a crocodile had bitten her face.

It took me a moment to process what I was seeing. Dainty legs wiggled underneath Nancy, and the girl—no older than sixteen—was begging her to get off. It reminded me of the 83-year-old Poppy who had tackled a murder suspect, Patricia Woodsbury, and then sat on top of her. Patricia had moved not a week after the whole ordeal, though it had little to do with her being tackled by Poppy and more to do with the fact that her cheating husband had been murdered. That was something her reputation would never recover from, and her reputation was all that mattered to her.

"Nance, what are you doing?" I said.

Bailey, her Boston Terrier, barked and jumped up at me, then went to join Nancy by sitting on the girl's legs.

"She was trying to steal a few candles," Eleanor said breathlessly. She had her thin hands placed over her heart and a look of sympathy in her eyes.

"Thief," Nancy said, as if that explained everything. Her platinum blonde hair was in the shape of a beehive, and she had a silk scarf around her head. She was dressed entirely in purple, even her lips matched.

Debating the best course of action, I looked around the group of women and realised they were the women belonging to the Castlefield Book Club, apart from Olivia, the baker's wife. Poppy was there, clutching the black handbag that she'd had since the sixties, as well as the Scottish Ava, who had no trouble saying what was on her mind in the bluntest way possible, though she was now quiet.

There was also Lily, whose cousin I had unmasked as a garden gnome thief a few years ago. She didn't much care for me, though I felt like there was the occasional moment of friendliness between us. Lily was also the inventor of useless items, such as dumbbells you could fill with water and that even came with a straw, or a hairbrush with a toothbrush attached to it, so you could simultaneously brush your hair and teeth. She had her greying blonde hair up, and her mouth was pinched, as if every word that came out of it was sour.

Phoebe and Jessica were also there, they were neighbours and usually at each other's throats over trivial matters. If not each other's, then someone else's. They always kept themselves busy with silly causes, though I suppose they weren't silly to them. A few weeks ago they had gone on a hunger strike because they didn't like the increased prices of bread. The hunger strike lasted twenty-six minutes.

All of the women were transfixed on the scene in front of them, even the usually calm and collected Eleanor. I had expected she would know what to do, but she just stared. Then, feeling my gaze, she looked up at me, her light eyes gaining clarity.

She cleared her throat. "The police have been called. Why don't you get off the poor girl, and we'll make sure she stays here until Alistair comes."

At the mere mention of Alistair my heart started beating faster.

"Don't overreact, now," Detective Black said in my ear.

"I won't," I muttered.

"What?" Eleanor said to me.

I shook my head.

"She's not a bloody poor girl," Nancy said. "She's a thief. Do you think we should give her some tea and biscuits while we're at it? Maybe give her my entire inventory, my bank card?"

"Tea would be lovely," the girl grunted from underneath Nancy.

I was about to tell Nancy to get up, when a low, smooth voice drew our attention.

"Everything alright, ladies?" Alistair was dressed in a three-piece suit like he was born in it. It hugged him in the right places, and somehow it didn't look too posh on him. He rarely wore anything else, and how he managed to move around in this heat without melting was beyond me and the universe.

His eyes immediately went to me, but he maintained a poker face and moved closer. "I take it this is not some sort of initiation for a new employee or something?"

Ava laughed. "If Nancy ever hired someone, then this would be the type of initiation she'd enjoy, no doubt. Maybe we should get her broom, so she can do some hitting."

This gathered a few chuckles from the ladies. Once my aunt hit someone with a broom because he was wearing Crocs.

Alistair held out his hand to Nancy. "Miss Knightley," he said in a gentle tone, yet the expression in his eyes was unyielding. They both stared at each other a moment. My aunt looked rather disappointed at the thought of not getting to crush this young woman any longer, but she grabbed his hand and he pulled her up, which elicited a groan from the teenager. Eleanor and Lily helped the girl to her feet. She still had one candle in her hand. The others were scattered about.

"Care to explain yourself, young lady?" he said in a fatherly tone.

The girl stuck out her bottom lip and fluttered her eyelids at him.

Did she really think that was going to work? I crossed my arms. "And the truth," I added.

She glanced at me as if she'd only just noticed me. She straightened her back and blew her black fringe out of her face. "Fine. I wanted some candles, and so I took them."

Nancy dashed forward, but Alistair was quicker. He held out his arm while Eleanor pulled her back. "Over my dead body," Nancy said.

The girl rolled her eyes. "Fine by me."

"Hey, don't talk to my aunt that way. You have no right to take what isn't yours. Especially for fun." I eyed her designer jeans. "What's your name?"

She narrowed her eyes at me. "Emblyn Cuff. What's yours?"

"Maggie Matthews. I own the bookshop next door. You've already met my aunt Nancy. She's not one to be trifled with."

"I like trifle," she said.

Eleanor smiled. She was the only person I knew who could smile and still look stern. "I make a very good one. Maybe I'll let you try some if you refrain from taking what doesn't belong to you."

The girl sighed dramatically. "It was a dare to myself, okay? I promise I won't do it again. Clearly I'm not very good at it."

"That's a good thing," Alistair said. "Trust me. Now, come on, I'll take you home."

At this her eyes widened. "No, please. My father is home, he'll kill me."

"I highly doubt that, besides, you should have thought about that before stealing. I think it's good that your parents are made aware of this." Alistair held out his arm. His eyes briefly went towards the curtain behind me, and I suspected Eddie had returned, but when I turned around, I saw that it was Christina. Emblyn followed him with another dramatic sigh. "On TV, detectives are way cooler," she said.

"I'll keep that in mind," Alistair said dryly.

As they passed Nancy, she yanked the last candle out of Emblyn's hand, and the girl stuck out her tongue. Nancy was about to have a go at her again, but this time me and Eleanor held her back. We watched them leave.

"Not a dull moment," Jessica said as she shook her head.

"Guess your cousin isn't the only thief in Castlefield," said Ava with a raw chuckle.

Lily glared at her and stuck her nose in the air. "I'll go and enjoy the first day of the Summer Festival, ladies." She sauntered off.

"Ah, don't be like that, pet," Ava said and followed her.

Jessica and Phoebe left soon as well, going straight for the ice cream truck. Poppy and Eleanor stayed behind with us.

"Are you okay?" I asked Nancy.

"Of course. I just don't like thieves. I just—can't stand them." She looked pale with anger.

"Why don't I make you a nice cup of tea," I said, because it was a fact that tea made everything better. Especially with biscuits.

Chapter 2

After Nancy had settled down, I took Christina to the village square which was overlooked by the vicarage. During the Summer Festival, the community garden at the vicarage was set up with several standing tables, and Olivia would bring baked goods to the vicar, Harold, who had volunteers help passing the treats around.

The square itself was filled with market stalls where the villagers could sell whatever they wanted for the next ten days. It was what drew in most visitors to our small Cornish village. Throughout the day and early evening we would have horseshoe throwing competitions. Tomorrow would be the writer's panel. The daily activities were a bonus; the best part was that we had a reason to all spend time together during these long summer days.

Christina and I walked past the ice cream truck—I was trying very hard not to eat too much since I still hadn't started working out—and headed to the first stalls. We passed people selling candles, wind chimes, and different kinds of chocolate which made my stomach growl.

I wanted to ask Christina if she was okay after seeing Alistair, but she was very focussed on all the items in front of us, so I didn't ask. I knew from personal experience that a broken heart required time to heal, and there were moments you wanted to talk about it and moments you wanted to pretend it had never happened. Whatever she needed, I would be there for her.

"Oh, look at those," she said as she pointed to small, delicate soaps with sweet scents that drew us closer.

"Hi, love," the woman owning the stall, Patty, said. She had a cute shop with all sorts of knick-knacks not too far from me. I had no idea she was into soaps, but I didn't frequent her shop much.

"These are very 'in,'" Christina said to me as she picked up a purple piece of soap and smelt it. She closed her eyes and moaned. "This is so good, smell." She pushed it under my nose.

It smelt like lavender and lilac. "It does smell good." To me, most soap smelt great, so paying four pounds for a tiny piece of soap made no sense, but Christina bought three different ones with a twinkle in her eyes.

We moved on and checked out the other stalls while the sun shone relentlessly on our heads. I realised I hadn't put sunscreen on, and I would probably end up with red shoulders and a red nose. It was the middle of July and the second week that the flat and my bookshop had needed air conditioning. The only thing that made this heat bearable was the excitement surrounding the Summer Festival. Although I didn't particularly like summer, I loved the togetherness that these next ten days brought out in Castlefield. Not that it wasn't already a close-knit community, but even more so with things like this.

Beth, our hundred-and-two-year-old resident, was also outside. She was sitting on a bench in the shade with Jessica and Phoebe on either side of her. They had bought her—and themselves—an ice cream and were doing their best to eat it before it melted.

Not far from them were four people who, after a moment, I recognised as the mystery authors I'd be doing a reading with tomorrow. I pointed them out to Christina.

"Well, let's go say hello. I'd love to find out if they're just as weird as you are." She giggled.

"I'm not that weird," I said.

"Last week you put a lot of ketchup on your hands and stomach, then walked around to check out the 'blood spatter.'" She raised her eyebrows.

"Ah, yes. That is weird," I said as we approached the group.

"Not to me," Detective Black muttered beside me.

"Hello, I don't know if you recognise me from our Skype session, but it's me, Maggie Matthews." I gave an awkward wave as I looked around the group. If four people were enough to make me nervous, I wasn't sure how I'd do at the reading tomorrow. In fact, I was dreading it, but it was part of my job.

"Ah, dear Maggie," the man named Carl Scranton said, as if we were long lost friends. He was chewing chewing gum, just like he had when we had Skyped. I recognised him by his bright copper hair and broad grin. During our collective Skype session he had also domineered the conversation. He was certainly not shy.

"An absolute delight to see your gorgeous self in person." He gave me a sticky kiss on my cheek that lasted a little too long for my liking and then planted one on Christina's. "And who are you?" he asked her.

"I—I'm Christina," she said.

"And Christina, these are the others," I said, as I pulled her away from Carl. He was a mystery author who had written only three books over the past twenty years, but they had been received relatively well. He had also won an award a few months ago, but I'd never heard of him until my agent mentioned him. My agent had also warned me that he had a tendency to flirt with anything that crossed his path. He was in his late forties, with an unnatural tan, and despite the blazing heat, he wore a cotton jacket and jeans. I didn't appreciate the way he was staring Christina up and down, and I had never wanted Pandora, the psycho chicken, by my side as much as then. I would gladly have picked her up and thrown her in his face.

Luckily, that wasn't necessary. There was another man around his mid-thirties, as well as a blonde woman of that same age and a younger one, in her early twenties. The blonde woman was named Wendy Cohen, and her husband and sometimes co-author Gregor Bykov had long dark hair that he had tied in a long braid. The young woman was named Sophia Taylor. She had black hair that was clearly dyed and some streaks were lighter, as if she'd missed them when colouring her hair.

We spent the next few minutes discussing the festival and Castlefield, and then we went on our way again. The group themselves split up as well, since Carl had spotted a group of lovely ladies to chat up. I wasn't sure if the other authors were relieved or not. They had all known him longer than I had. Apparently, they were part of the same writing group. I had considered joining one of those once, but realised I had enough trouble dealing with Detective Black's comments about my writing.

"Well, then," he said, "learn when to place commas, and I'll leave you alone."

ABOUT AN HOUR LATER I was fed up with the scorching sun that was trying to burn me alive, so I headed back in the direction of the shop. Christina had already returned twenty minutes earlier to relieve Eddie from his bookshop duties, so he could have a long break. He was throwing horseshoes with Sophia. She was giggling at something he said, and it could have been due to the sun, but I was fairly certain he was blushing. I smiled at the sight as I kept walking and bumped into someone.

"So sorry," I muttered and stared into Alistair's eyes.

"No problem." He smiled at me, his hands in his pockets. "Having fun?"

Detective Black popped up next to me. "Play it cool. Definitely don't think about his lips."

"Yes, it's a lip—I mean lovely first day of the Summer Festival. Not much has changed since we were teens, huh?" I said and cleared my throat, hoping he hadn't noticed my slip-up.

"I suspect only we have changed." He looked around, then back at me. "How are you?" His voice was soft, his stare penetrative.

"I'm fine. Business as usual. How are you?"

His dark eyes scanned my face. "Good. I'm doing...good."

We stared at each other. The space between us slowly filled with the unsaid, like a balloon about to burst.

Alistair broke the silence. "Do you think—" He was interrupted by the sound of Pandora's battle cry and the screams of innocent Summer Festival goers.

We turned to see the red chicken chasing two middle-aged women with shopping bags.

"Excuse me," Alistair said. He ran to the nearest market stall that was selling wicker baskets and straw brooms. He picked up one of the brooms and dashed to the other side of the market from where the women ran our way, shrieking as Pandora chased them with fluttering wings. She really was evil. She probably slept on the bones of her defeated enemies.

"Hey," the owner of the stall called, but as he watched Alistair run over to Pandora, he followed the scene with interest. Just like many others who stopped what they were doing to see if the detective would survive the oncoming blood bath.

The women ran on while Alistair reached them and moved the broom out in front of Pandora's path. She tried to jump over it, but Alistair moved it up as well and gently brushed her back. She let out a shriek and tried to go for his legs. He anticipated that move with the broom and blocked her. This went on for a while. It was like watching a chicken dance with a broom. Eventually she became bored and stalked off.

The locals, who knew all too well how terrorising Pandora could be, started clapping. The two women who had been on the run from her homicidal tendencies returned to Alistair to thank him. He stood there holding the broom as he chatted with them.

"Wow, he really is something," the man from the broom stall said.

"He is," I said.

"Maybe you should throw some cold water over yourself," Detective Black said.

"That would be nice, considering the fact that the sun is trying to melt me."

"What?" the man from the stall asked.

"I don't like Alistair. What? Nothing." I dashed off to the The Wicked Bookworm where there was air conditioning, which I desperately needed. I was clearly becoming delirious. Alistair watched me go. It was probably best if we didn't get too chummy.

LATER THAT EVENING Christina and I had dinner at the pub. During the Summer Festival it was always busy in The Rose, but we found a spot by the half-open window. It was still light out, but there was a gentle breeze that occasionally made the ivy on the side of the pub tremble.

Eddie was by the bar with Sophia, so I guess they hit it off today. The other two mystery authors were on the other side of the bar, chatting, while Carl was entertaining a group of people. He was too far away for me to hear what he was discussing, but he made wild gestures and occasionally a roar of laughter emerged from those who were hanging from his lips.

We ordered food from Callum, who was dressed stylishly as ever in his bow tie and silk shirt. It was too busy for him to be texting his new boyfriend, a professional skier from Canada, but otherwise that was exactly what he'd be doing. He was only working at the pub to pay for his acting lessons. One day he'd leave Castlefield, become famous and forget us all.

When Eddie spotted us, he came over and brought Sophia along. "Hi, guys. Have you met Sophia yet?" he asked.

She gave us a smile. "Yes, I've met them already."

"Sit down." I pulled out the chair next to me, so that Eddie could sit down. "How are you enjoying your first day in Castlefield?" I asked once they were settled.

"It is such a cute village. The cottages are beautiful, and so is the scenery. I was a bit nervous about tomorrow, but everyone is so nice, I'm looking forward to it now."

I wish I could have said the same. I was still dreading having all those eyes on me. It was just easier dealing with fictional people. Not that I expected anything bad to happen, but technically there was the possibility that people would start laughing at me. Or maybe Pandora would terrorise the crowd and chase everyone away.

"I'm glad you're enjoying yourself. I hope Eddie has been good to you." I grinned at him.

He kicked me under the table as his face adopted the colour of a tomato.

Sophia chuckled while Christina bit her lip, presumably to stop herself from laughing.

"He has been very nice, indeed," Sophia said and flashed Eddie a smile. If she kept it up, he would become so red he could stop traffic.

"Your first book recently got published, didn't it?" I asked in order to make conversation. I already knew this from our Skype session.

"Yes, that's right. It's about a female private investigator who solves a string of murders." And she continued to tell us more about it. Eddie seemed interested in everything she said and nodded enthusiastically every now and then.

There was another burst of laughter from the group that Carl was sitting with. We all looked up.

"He sure likes talking, doesn't he?" I said to Sophia.

"Yeah. He loves attention. Which is also why he's so excited for tomorrow. I also don't think his latest book did so well." Her cheeks reddened. "I'm sorry. That was mean."

"No, not at all," Eddie said. "Not if it's simply a fact."

"Even so." She shrugged.

"Are you close with Carl? Are the others?"

"Wendy and Gregor have known him for a while. I met him about two months ago. When my book was published I wanted to join a local author's club, and that's how I met them. We basically help each other brainstorm, or sometimes beta read each other's work. It's more like a support group." She laughed.

It sounded nice, not that I needed a club like that, I already had my support group.

"And where are you from?" Christina asked.

"Devon."

Eddie and Sophia also ordered dinner, and we stayed for another hour, but the pub got busier, and I had promised to help Harold. Yesterday around this time, I had helped him put up balloons on the gate around the cemetery. Today I would help him hang up birdhouses. Every few years he'd hang up new ones, not because there was anything wrong with them, but because he liked building them. He painted doors and windows on, though I doubted the bright colours would attract the birds. Not that it mattered; it brought him joy.

I left the others at the pub for a drink while I went outside. As I headed toward the vicarage I heard footsteps behind me. I picked up the pace, but so did the person behind me.

"You really should start carrying weapons. Maybe bring a broom with you," Detective Black said.

Someone touched my arm.

I swung my handbag around, but it got blocked by the person's arm. It happened too quick for me to see who it was, but I kicked him.

"Ouch, Maggie. It's me," Alistair said. He hopped on one leg as I lowered my handbag. "Does being violent run in your family?"

I chuckled. "Oops. Sorry."

He rubbed his leg and stood up straight. "No, I'm sorry. I didn't mean to scare you."

"That's okay. Now I got to show off my fighting skills. I could be an extra in an action film."

He laughed. "Yes, you'd be kicking bad guys' butts with your handbag."

"Don't mock the handbag, it's how Nancy lost her eye."

His mouth fell open. "Really?"

Now it was my turn to laugh. "No."

"How *did* it happen?"

"That depends on what mood she is in when you ask her. Will you walk me to the vicarage?"

"Of course." We continued to walk side by side. It was significantly cooler now, though still warm.

"I liked the way you handled Pandora today," I said to him.

"Yes, well, we couldn't have her attack those poor women. I still can't believe a chicken can do so much damage. Maybe I should arrest her and scare her straight."

I laughed as I pictured Pandora in handcuffs. "How did it go with that girl, Emblyn?"

"Her dad is some hotshot businessman. He barely gave her the time of day. He said she was grounded for a month and then took a phone call. I think the girl was acting out to get his attention. I saw that a lot when I was in uniform. Parents have a great influence on the behaviour of their children."

I swallowed. In my case I hoped my mother had as little influence on me as possible. It wasn't her fault she had mental issues, of course, but she had caused certain scars that weren't so easy to heal.

"Are you excited for tomorrow?" he asked after a moment of silence.

"Yea—err, no. I'm nervous." I bit my lip as I thought about standing there in front of those people.

"What are you nervous about?"

"Just all those people staring at me. And don't tell me to picture them naked, that would be even worse."

He chuckled. "Yeah, that advice doesn't work. What you could do is smile and force yourself to look around at the faces. Then you'll see that it's really just people looking at you, nothing more, nothing less. Then you focus on what you're reading while occasionally glancing in the direction of someone you don't mind looking at. Someone you feel comfortable with. A lot of friends will be part of the audience, so you can use that. If I were you, I wouldn't be too worried. One smile from you, and they'll all be putty in your hands."

I looked at him. "That's very sweet of you."

"Just being honest," he said.

We reached the gate to the vicarage. "I appreciate it."

"That's what friends are for. Right?" His eyes searched mine. The answer was clearly important to him.

The smart thing was to say that he wasn't my friend. At least, not until Christina was officially over her broken heart.

Not to mention that I wasn't sure if we could be friends; I was attracted to him. Being close to him would only mess with my head.

I smiled at him. I would let him down gently.

"Yes, we are."

Damn it.

"Yes, you really let him down easy," Detective Black said with an eye roll.

Chapter 3

Harold had built and painted three new birdhouses. He had made one look like a mansion and even painted a fountain on the front. It was unnecessary, but he enjoyed doing it. He had tiny brushes and a lot of patience. He moved swiftly in his wheelchair even if the grass wasn't the easiest to navigate. He had two birdhouses on his lap, while I carried the other one. I put it down on the ground by the oak tree at the edge of the cemetery and removed the older birdhouse. They would be added to Gil's market stall; he sold antiques and objects crafted by talented members of the community.

"If I ever decide to move into a cottage, make sure you get me one too," I said as I bent down to pick up the new birdhouse. It smelt of paint.

He chuckled. "I'll make you one that looks like The Wicked Bookworm."

"No way, that would be so cool," I said as my eyes widened. "I might want to live in it myself."

"That might be a good idea. I don't think the birds do. It's just that I like making these birdhouses, and they look cute."

I hung up the first house and took a step back to admire it. "Well, you're right about that."

We continued hanging up the other two houses and then joined Eleanor in their back garden with lush rosebushes and other plants and flowers. The garden was thriving in the summer heat and bees and butterflies were frequent visitors. Eleanor had put out lemonade and lemon tarts. The sky was turning pink as the sun was setting.

"How did you enjoy your first day of the Summer Festival?" Eleanor asked. She was wearing a summer dress with white flowers. Only during summer did she wear dresses, even though they looked so good on her. Her other outfits were a lot more reserved and bland. Not too long ago my wardrobe could have been hers. I was glad I was putting in more effort into my clothes, shoes, and even handbags. Not that I was doing that for anybody else. Not even for Alistair.

"In fact," Detective Black said, startling me. "I believe he called you perfect once."

I felt my cheeks get warm and was sure I was blushing.

"It was fine," I said and took a sip of the cold drink.

"Alistair had a stand-off with Pandora, I heard." She smiled. "He also walked Beth and Poppy home. He advised them to drink lots of fluids in this warm weather and even bought them a lot of water bottles. Delivered them right to their doorstep with DC Daniels."

"Really?" I asked.

"He seems like a good man," Harold said.

Eleanor studied my face. She knew all about what had happened to us when he first moved back.

"He is," I said. And he was. He was also very human and had made some bad decisions, but so had I.

"Speaking of good men." Harold cleared his throat.

"Oh, boy," Detective Black said.

Harold only did that when he had something serious to discuss. The last time he cleared his throat was when he wanted to discuss the dangers of cycling with untied shoelaces. Apparently he had witnessed someone fall off his bike and right into Pandora, who had seen it as a full frontal assault. It ended with a trip to the hospital for the poor bloke. He hadn't stopped cycling, but he had become a strict vegetarian after that.

"I met this really nice man when I went to visit a family in Green Field; the mother is an old friend of mine. He ended a relationship about six months ago, and we chatted about how difficult it is to find someone interesting these days. These were his experiences, not mine." He winked at Eleanor, and she giggled. "But it's something I hear a lot, including from you."

I see where this is going. Towards the edge of a cliff.

"Listen—" I started.

"You just say the word, and I'll give you his number. If you don't ask for it, that's also fine. Now, have a lemon tart." He winked at me.

I couldn't say no to that. The tart, not the phone number.

IT WAS DARK BY THE time I returned to my flat. Christina was on the sofa with Snowball. She was trying to teach her to come when she called her name. Apparently bunnies could be taught to do tricks. I had seen videos. It was amazing.

"Hey," I said and plopped down next to her. "Today was fun, huh?"

Christina picked up Snowball and snuggled with her. "Yeah. Listen, I need a favour." Her voice had gone up, and she refused eye contact.

I swallowed.

"See, this is what happens when you're too social," Detective Black said. "People are nothing but trouble. You should be writing. I want to solve a murder."

"What is it?" I asked.

"First of all, I want to thank you for letting me wallow and get over Alistair. I really appreciate it. I'm very close to being over him, I just need one more thing. And I think only you can help me."

I waited.

"Don't ask me how I know this, but every Wednesday Alistair leaves the house for an hour and then comes back. The thing is, I have the feeling that maybe he cheated on me right before breaking things off with me. I think he might be seeing that woman every Wednesday. I need you to find out if it's true. Be a sleuth again." She glanced at me, gauging my reaction.

"You don't want me to ask him, you want me to follow him and find out where he goes?"

"Yes." She bit her lip. "I know you must think I'm terrible for asking this, but he was acting so weird before we broke up. He stopped being...you know, physical with me when moving here."

"Gag," Detective Black said. "Too much information."

I rubbed my temple. "I—I don't know."

"Please, I need to know."

I contemplated telling her about the almost-kiss, but decided against it. What if I had imagined the vibes he'd thrown me? What if she was right, and he was seeing someone? What if he was a cheater just like my ex?

Don't think like that. But it was too late.

"I'll do it," I said.

She beamed at me. "Great. I'm so lucky to have you."

"And I'm lucky to have you." I fished out a pocket knife.

Her eyes widened. "Oh oh."

I wiggled my eyebrows. "I found this at the market today. I'm going to keep it on me, just like Detective Black will once I start writing chapter five. Anyway, I need you to tie me up again. I want to see if it works."

"That's just the thing to do on a Monday night," she said while a smile tugged on her lips.

"What can I say? Writers are weird."

THE NEXT MORNING I got up early to get some writing done. It had taken me six and a half minutes to get out of the rope, and it had given me extra motivation to write. Detective Black was going to get into trouble, and I was looking forward to it.

"Sadist," he muttered next to me.

I finished one and a half chapter by noon and had a piece of toast before heading down to the bookshop. Christina and Eddie were working. They wouldn't be attending the reading, but that was alright. I didn't want to close The Wicked Bookworm and lose potential customers. The Summer Festival brought a lot of extra sales.

Just as I was about to head out, Miles Mortimer strode in. He was dressed in a white shirt and khaki shorts. I met him when I got into trouble with the law, and he was friends with Alistair. He'd recently moved into the Pembroke because apparently he liked living in a cursed deathtrap of a place. Not to mention, people had died there. The Pembroke Hotel was built by a serial killer. But no, instead of buying a cute cottage, he had to buy that awful place. Okay, it was beautiful, but Alistair and I had nearly died there, not to mention Victor Woodsbury actually had.

Miles shot me his dazzling smile when he saw me and ran a hand through his light-blond hair. In a way, he reminded me of Alistair. They both valued their appearances and aimed to look professional. They were childhood friends, and Miles had grown up in Castlefield but then moved away. Now he was back and though he seemed nice, I hadn't spent much time with him.

"The always gorgeous Maggie," Miles said as he approached me. "How are you?"

"It's probably a good thing you haven't met my aunt yet. If you greeted her like that, she'd probably hit you with a kettle."

He raised an eyebrow and looked around, as if she would jump out at him any second. "I'll keep that in mind. Listen, I have a massive library filled with books that aren't mine. Some of them are quite old, some are new. You can have whichever you like, or donate those you don't, I don't care. I'd like to fill it with my own books, renovate it so it becomes a study that will actually be used. Will you help? You can just show up whenever you want, there's no deadline."

I frowned. "Are you planning on opening the Pembroke as a hotel again?" This was something the entire village wanted to know. Miles didn't hang out at the pub, and I was certain he'd hired someone to do his shopping for him, so nobody saw much of him.

"Not anytime soon. First I want to make it my own. I've only just finished renovating the bits that were damaged by the fire."

The fire that had killed Mr Field. Another one to add to the death list. "Are you sure you wouldn't rather live somewhere less...homicidal?"

He chuckled. "The past is the past, dear. It's a beautiful place that deserves to be treated well, not shunned because of what people did in it. Besides, don't you believe in second chances?"

That was a good question, and I couldn't help but think about my mother. She rang me a couple of days ago, and according to my aunt, she was doing well enough to leave the mental hospital soon. It had been a long time since I'd seen her, and I preferred it that way. Still, some nights I'd lie awake and think about what it could be like. A version where we were all happy, together. "I believe in second chances," I said. "Just not more than that. But I'm glad you're not opening it to the public, it might keep the death count steady."

"I do plan on that." He smirked. "So are you in?"

"I'm in. I can't resist books. And food."

He chuckled. "Good, I'll make sure there will be both." He handed me a key. "You're welcome to let yourself in any time. Don't give that key to anyone else, though. Obviously."

"Got it." I immediately put it on my key chain and slipped it back into my yellow handbag. It stood out against my red dress. "Will you check out the reading today?"

"I'll probably check it out. No promises. I abhor the heat."

"Me too. I put on two extra layers of sunscreen, but by the time the Mystery Readings are over, I'll probably still be red as a lobster." I made a face.

"It would match your dress," he said.

"Glad you're looking on the bright side. I've got to go and make preparations. See you."

"Bye."

I left him behind in the bookshop and headed outside where the heat hit me like a brick wall. I had to resist the urge to run back inside where there was air conditioning. It was slightly warmer than yesterday, and I was certain the universe was out to get me.

The Mystery Readings would last about two hours since we'd also be doing signings. Harold and Eleanor had summoned volunteers during this Summer Festival to help out.

Tomorrow, for instance, me and the half of the Castlefield Book Club would help out with the pie eating contest. Today Stanley, the baker, and a bunch of his mates had set up the table for the signings. They had provided a sheet that functioned as a parasol. But the actual readings were on a wooden platform with one microphone and five wooden chairs placed in a row. There was no protection from the sun. I should have put on a hat.

Plastic chairs had been put out in front of the platform. There were enough for an audience of about sixty people. Others could stand. I wasn't sure how many people would show up to this. This was the first year we were doing something like this.

All I could do was hope it would be a success.

"Besides," Detective Black said, "what's the worst that can happen? It won't kill you, will it?"

I glared at him. "Don't you dare jinx this."

A scream filled the air.

Chapter 4

The scream had come from the table set up for our signings. The stacks of books had already been brought out, as well as our name tags, and plenty of pens. The four authors were there as well, since we'd start in about twenty minutes. Nothing seemed out of the ordinary; nobody was on the ground or appeared hurt. Yet Wendy had her arm around Sophia, and Gregor came up to her with a bunch of napkins.

Sophia turned for a brief moment, and I gasped. There was blood coming out of her nose. A lot of it. Part of her dress was covered in it. A crowd was starting to gather. DC Daniels showed up by her side with an ice cream cone. Ice cream was dripping over his hand.

I rushed forward. She was about my size and my flat was close. She clearly needed a new dress and some privacy. "Here, we'll go to my place."

"She's bleeding a lot," George said. "Should we call an ambulance?"

She shook her head. "It's just a bloody nose." Her voice was muffled because of the napkins pressed against her nose and mouth.

"I'll take her. It will be fine."

Carl was leaning against the table and had a peculiar look on his face. He was the only one not panicking, but he also showed no concern whatsoever.

I wrapped my arm around Sophia and headed to the bookshop. Eddie rushed over as soon as we stepped inside. "What the hell happened? Are you okay?"

"She's fine. She just needs some space. I'll get her upstairs, clean her up. All will be well. Please stay here." The last thing we both needed was a panicked Eddie.

The people who were in the shop followed us with interest. From the corner of my eye I spotted Miles chatting with Christina and Eleanor. They hadn't seen us yet as they were in the far corner and engaged in conversation.

I used the back door, and we went up the stairs to the flat. "This way," I said and directed her to my bathroom. I helped her take off her dress and luckily, by that time, the bleeding had stopped. I cleaned the blood with wet towels and then put her in one of my dresses; a purple one that brought out her eyes. While she was undressing, I observed several small bruises on her arms and legs.

"I hope those bruises weren't caused by a person," I said. It was none of my business, but the sight worried me.

She glanced at me over her shoulder and flashed me a smile. "No, I just always bump into things and sometimes I'll even have bruises when I wake up, not knowing how I got them. Don't worry about it, I'm used to it."

I sighed with relief. At least it was nice to know I wasn't the only clumsy person. I had a massive bruise on my leg after I bumped into the corner of the coffee table the other day. I also had the uncanny ability to pass an open door and hit my arm on the door handle.

"So the nose bleed, does that happen often?" I asked.

"No, but this morning I fell out of bed and hit my nose, maybe that's why it started bleeding."

Detective Black popped up next to me. "I don't think that can happen."

"Thank you for the dress. It fits me nicely." She turned around.

The fabric hung loose around her hips and chest, but it was only noticeable if you paid close attention.

"I'll get it back to you as soon as possible," she said.

"Are you okay enough to get on with the show?" She looked a bit pale, but otherwise fine.

"Absolutely."

Downstairs she chatted briefly with Eddie, assuring him that she was fine. By now, Eleanor and Miles were gone, and Christina was helping a customer. I checked my watch. We were going to be late. I dragged Sophia away from Eddie, and just as we were about to leave, Pandora was in front of the entrance, staring us down.

She must have been attracted by the scent of blood and was now hungry for more.

I grabbed Sophia's hand. "Let's go through my aunt's store."

"What?" She glanced at Pandora, before I pulled her along. "It's just a chicken."

"Ha, just a chicken. Famous last words, sweetheart. That is not just a chicken," I said as we went into my aunt's store. Nancy was showing a customer how to do a rain dance. It looked like she had ants in her pants.

We were about to head out through the front entrance, when Pandora was there as well. Still staring.

"She's been sent from the depths of hell to torment us." I stared back.

Sophia laughed, then looked into Pandora's eyes. She turned serious, then shivered. "Okay, I think I believe you."

Just as I was about to return to the back room to get Nancy's broom, Pandora glanced behind her and shot off in the other direction. When I looked up, Alistair strode over.

"Are you girls okay? Did the mean chicken scare you?" He grinned at me.

"You survive one battle with demonic poultry and all of a sudden you think you're the man, huh?" I put my hand on Sophia's back. "Let's go."

Alistair sniggered.

The seats in front of the small self-made stage were filled as we arrived. The mystery authors were already on their wooden chairs. I was going to introduce them and start off with my reading, so it was show time.

My stomach fluttered as if I'd swallowed butterflies with ADD. I checked to make sure the authors were ready, grabbed a copy of my latest novel, which was on my chair, and stood in front of the microphone.

Okay, stay calm, Maggie. This is going to be fine. Except for if I forget words. Like, all of them. And that can't happen, so it will be fine.

I managed a smile. "Hilo," I said. *Damn it.*

"It helps to pick either 'hi' or 'hello,'" Detective Black said and snorted.

Nobody in the audience made a sound, much to my relief. I glanced around, remembering Alistair's advice. I found him in the audience, standing to the side. He had taken his sunglasses off, though he had to hold his hand up to shield himself from the sun. He smiled at me.

I also spotted the book club ladies, and even Olivia had left the bakery to come look. It helped. "I'm Maggie Matthews and with me today are four other mystery authors. Which means that for the first time you're looking at people who have committed a lot of murders. At least, I hope it's your first time."

There was a short chuckle from the crowd.

I introduced the other authors, their latest books, and then told them about mine. I started reading a passage where Detective Black talks to a widow who lets him know she's the killer, but without explicitly saying it. It is a tense scene.

Afterwards the audience applauded. There was a loud whistle from Eleanor, and Alistair followed suit. I smiled and took a bow, then sat down on my chair while Carl got up. He tapped his book and then sauntered over to the microphone, as if he was enjoying all those eyes on him and wanted to drag it out as long as possible.

He cleared his throat and started talking about himself and his books. Instead of a brief intro, he took about six minutes to do this. Several people yawned.

Finally, he opened his book and started reading a passage. He chose to read the passage where the detective finds the body. He only got three lines in when someone in the audience shouted.

"Thief!" A woman with a dark, long braid stood up. She was in her mid-to-late forties. "You stole my manuscript, that is my story."

The crowd started murmuring.

Why did this have to happen now? The first thing I organise, and bam, trouble. Alistair had started moving forward in case she'd make her way over to us. This way he could intercept her.

Carl continued reading.

"Thief. You don't have a creative bone in your body, you charlatan." She was at the edge of the seats so it wasn't difficult for her to approach us. Except that Alistair got there first.

"Miss, I'm going to have to ask you to sit down or leave. You're disturbing the peace," he said in a professional tone. He had switched to police mode.

"Disturbing the peace? He's disturbing justice."

I got up and told Carl to keep reading, which he did, while I made my way over to her. "I hear you," I said to her, calmly. "And I'd like to hear what you have to say, follow me." I glanced at Alistair to signal for him to come as well, just in case she was deranged.

They both followed me to the church where it was cool inside and quiet. There was a family of tourists with cameras around their necks, who were just leaving. We were the only ones.

I wasn't sure if she was telling the truth, but she was obviously upset, and the best way to get her to calm down was to listen and validate her feelings. "What is your name?" I asked. "I'm Maggie."

"Rachel. Rachel Farris. I met him in a writing class. We hit it off. We even had a brief fling." She blushed at this. "I told him about a story I was working on, and he helped me brainstorm. We talked about it a lot. I typed the manuscript on my computer. He broke it off with me around the time I finished the manuscript. Then he disappeared, changed his number. He had also deleted the manuscript. I didn't realise that at first. Thought it was just my computer malfunctioning. But then his book came out. It had a different title, but everything else was the same. Everything!" She burst into tears.

Alistair and I exchanged a glance.

"I'm so sorry. That must have been terrible," I said.

"It still is. He is getting credit and money for something I wrote. It's ridiculous. It's unfair." She stomped her foot in anger and glanced at the cross at the end of the church. "Don't you worry, though. He'll get what's coming to him. Justice will be served, and he will be punished." Then she stormed out of the church, leaving only a delicate flowery scent behind.

"That always leads to murder," Detective Black said.

Alistair sighed. "That was...interesting."

"The first reading I organise and someone gets threatened. Publicly."

"Hey, you did great," he said and put his hand on my shoulder. "Everybody was riveted. You chose a good piece to read out. You're a talented author."

He sure knew what to say. I smiled at him. "Thank you." There was applause, which meant that Carl was done. "We better get out there," I said. "And hope there's no more drama."

THE REST OF THE READING went without any hiccups. The longest queue for autographs was right in front of me, but that was not surprising since I was the local mystery author. It didn't mean that the others weren't doing well, but still Carl huffed and puffed and glared at me.

Afterwards, the other authors enjoyed the festival while I retreated to Nancy's for a sandwich. I made one for her as well and brought it down, so we could eat it at the counter. Nancy pretty much never left her shop, not even for lunch.

I was about to take a bite out of my cheese sandwich when I spotted a golden necklace around her neck. It was simple and elegant. Something she'd never wear. In fact, she only wore silver jewellery and hated the look of gold. Said it was tacky.

"Where'd you get that necklace?" I asked, pretending to be focussed on my lunch.

She froze for the briefest of moments. "Nowhere."

I raised my eyebrow.

"I mean," she said, "I found it here. And I'm wearing it in case the woman returns for it. Then she'll see it on me and know where it is."

"Interesting."

She glared at me. "Yes, I'm a good person that way. I'm just doing my civic duty in helping some poor woman find her necklace. That is all."

I laughed. "Sure, you stick with that story."

She was about to open her mouth when Rachel, the woman who had accused Carl, walked in. She smiled apologetically at me and seemed more composed.

"I just wanted to apologise for earlier. I spoke to the vicar's wife, and she let me know you were the one that set the whole thing up. If I ruined anything, I'm sorry. Though I don't regret accosting him, I do regret doing it at that time. It felt like the right thing to do, to expose him in public," she said.

"I missed drama?" Nancy asked. "Why didn't you tell me I missed drama?"

I made a dismissive gesture, then turned to the woman. "Don't worry, Rachel. I understand your frustration. What are you going to do next?"

"I'm going to try and talk to him. I got a room at the B&B. Carl, however, is staying at the Pembroke Hotel."

"He is?" Nancy and I said simultaneously.

"But it's not a hotel, not right now," I said.

She shrugged. "That's what the other authors said."

Nancy and I exchanged a glance.

"Anyway, sorry again. Please take care."

"You as well. Be careful," I said.

She smiled and then left.

Nancy looked at me. "Well? Are you waiting for a written invitation? Spill."

THAT NIGHT CHRISTINA and I went over to the pub for a drink. We'd had dinner at home to avoid the rush, but it was still busy at The Rose. We found a spot just as a couple was leaving. I sat down while Christina got us drinks. She returned shortly with white wine for her and a lemonade for me.

Soon she was sharing stories about horrible first dates she'd had. I laughed when she described a man who took her to see his dead butterfly collection. I could just picture the look on her face.

My attention was suddenly drawn to the bar. Alistair was looking at me. I hadn't seen him when we came in. I gave him a smile, then focussed on Christina. I didn't want her to follow my gaze; I wasn't sure if she could relax with him right there.

The door banged open, and Carl walked in. "I've got it," he said, and held up a statuette of a quill in an ink jar.

A group near the door applauded.

"I told you I had it. I earned this prize, along with this fountain pen," he said and tapped his breast pocket. He still held the statuette up triumphantly. He spoke loudly and gathered the attention of others within earshot. "I earned this prize because I'm a good writer. Don't let anybody tell you differently. I'm also very, very good in bed."

This elicited a few shocked gasps and giggles.

I rolled my eyes and inwardly gagged.

"Why do men always feel the need to boast?" Christina asked.

"Yeah, you don't see Poppy rushing into the pub holding up her newly knitted scarf, calling herself a great knitter."

Christina laughed at that image.

Carl turned around and caught her eye. "Do you think that's funny?"

He made his way over to us, and I instinctively got up to block his path to Christina. He was harmless, I was sure, but I didn't like the look in his eyes.

From the corner of my eye I could see Alistair had gotten up as well; he was now a few steps away.

"Perhaps it's time to leave," I said firmly.

"Or get punched," Detective Black said.

"You think you're all that, don't you, little girl?" he said. "Well, I've read your latest novel, and it's shite!"

This time a lot of people gasped.

"Punch him, punch him hard," Detective Black said.

"Okay, that's it. I'm kicking you out," Alistair said and walked around the nearest table to get to him.

Again the door burst open. A man I didn't recognise stood in the doorway. His eyes went to Carl. "You," he said and pointed at him. The man looked like he went to the gym and was a foot taller than Carl. "Have you been flirting with my wife?"

Carl shrugged. "I flirt with a lot of women, can't remember all their names. Or faces. Or cup sizes."

That did it.

In one swift motion the man punched Carl right in the face, and he flew back into the table next to us. It toppled over, along with Carl. He was ready to dive on top of him again, but Alistair and a few other villagers held the man back and wrestled him out of the pub while Carl was on the ground, groaning.

"Never a dull moment in Castlefield," Christina muttered.

Chapter 5

That Wednesday morning I was outside Alistair's cottage. I felt like I was invading his privacy just standing there, which was also why I had no intention of following him. I would do the normal thing and ask him. Just because Christina didn't want to, didn't mean I couldn't. She'd asked me to find out the truth, and that was what I would do. I rang the doorbell.

He opened the door and smiled when he saw it was me. When I didn't smile back, he frowned. "What's wrong?"

"Nothing, I—can I come in?"

"Of course." He stepped aside.

"Thank you."

A moment later we were at his kitchen table. He had offered me tea, but I had declined. He probably had to leave soon. I sighed. "Christina wanted me to follow you this morning."

"What?" He frowned. "Why?"

"Because she knows you leave every Wednesday morning, and she thinks you're having an affair. She thinks you've been having an affair ever since you got here."

He scoffed. "That's ridiculous."

"Is it?"

His dark eyes searched my face, and he shifted in his seat. "Tell her I'm not."

"So you're not about to meet with a woman, then?"

"I am, but not for the reason she thinks. Or you, apparently. I mean, do you really think I'd do that?" He leaned forward.

"We almost kissed," I said, not meeting his eyes.

"Yes, but we didn't. Besides I didn't plan on kissing you, you just—" his voice trailed off. "You didn't tell her about it, did you?"

"Do you care if I did?"

"Of course. You're friends. It might ruin your friendship with her. I don't want that."

I raised my eyebrows. Did he really not want her to know just for my sake? "So you wouldn't care if she got upset with you?"

He bit his lip. A sexy gesture. "Of course I don't want to hurt her, but I already have. I also realise that my relationship with her was bad for me. That's actually related to where I'm going each Wednesday morning. I'm seeing a psychologist. For my life, my work, just everything." He sighed. "I've been trying to make a beautiful image with puzzle pieces that didn't quite fit, now I have to undo it all and look at the big picture. Look at what I want." His eyes met mine.

I swallowed, suddenly feeling hot. "I see. That's very good of you," I said and looked away.

"Anyway, I'll talk to her."

"You will?" I looked back at him.

"Yes. She clearly needs closure. I ended things very abruptly. Thanks for telling me about this." He got up and checked his watch. "I should get going. Are you and Christina okay after what happened last night?"

I got up as well. "Yes. It was odd, though, wasn't it? He seems like a man who cares very much about what others think of him, and who wants to be adored, but at the same time he appears shallow. The other authors had said that he's staying with Miles. Is that true, do you know?"

He shook his head. "He's not. I had dinner with Miles yesterday. It's just him, and occasionally maids come in to clean or Kelly shows up with groceries. He would have told me if he had a guest."

"I wonder where he's staying then."

"We could ask him," he said, "if you think it matters."

"We? Do you smell a mystery, Watson?"

"I'm pretty sure I'm Sherlock, and I doubt it's a mystery."

"No, I'm Sherlock, and it is a mystery, even if it's a small one."

Alistair smiled.

I smiled back.

"Whatever you want," he said, but in a sweet way, as if he'd give me the world on a silver platter if I asked.

I felt my cheeks get hot. "I should go. We have the pie contest preparations. Will you be there? First we have the pie contest to select the tastiest pie, then we'll have the pie eating contest with the pies that don't win. The winner wins the best pie."

"Yes, I know. I've entered the pie eating contest."

My jaw dropped. "You have? So have I."

He smirked. "Well, well, well, look at that. I guess we'll be competing then. Tell you what, if you finish faster than me, you get to call yourself Sherlock. If I am faster than you, I get that title." He held out his hand.

"Deal," I said and shook it.

HALF OF THE CASTLEFIELD Book Club, and myself, had gathered at Stan's Bakery where Olivia had the pies ready. They were all made by different villagers who had volunteered, but Olivia stored them in her big fridge. My mouth began to water at the sight.

"Down, girl, you'll get your chance at the pie eating competition," Detective Black said.

I had purposely eaten only a cracker, which was not allowed to be called food, in my opinion. It was basically just pretentious air that was chewable. My stomach grumbled. I wasn't sure if I'd make it through. If I happened across Pandora, I might be forced to eat her.

Olivia led the way with a cart on wheels that held all the cakes. It was difficult to get over the cobbled street, but Eleanor and I helped her while Phoebe, Lily, and Jessica trailed behind us.

"What an ordeal yesterday," Lily said behind us. "I wasn't there myself, but I heard it was quite the scene. I'm not surprised that Maggie was involved," she added maliciously.

"I know, Maggie always knows how to handle such situations," Phoebe said, unaware of Lily's sneaky insult.

"What exactly happened?" Poppy asked. She never hung out at the pub.

"Carl Scranton, the mystery writer with the copper hair, was making a scene at the pub," I said over my shoulder. "It's really not a big deal. We shouldn't blow it up too much."

Carefully we made our way to the church and headed up the path to the wooden door. It was still early in the morning but the heat was building up, like a sauna. I was relieved we'd spent most of the time inside of the cool church today.

"I'll get the door," I said and opened it for them while Olivia and Eleanor pushed the cart inside. The table had already been set up in the back of the church where the pies would be placed, and later it would be moved to the front of the church, which had an elevated platform, and gave everyone a good view of the contestants stuffing their faces. And I would be one of them. I was excited already. Eating one pie was nothing; I'd once eaten a whole pie as dessert. It was kind of an accident. I had been so captivated by an episode of *Silent Witness* that it was gone before I realised it.

Poppy tugged on my sleeve while the others set up.

"What?" I turned to her.

"Is that man supposed to lie there?" She pointed.

I followed her gaze. At the front of the church was a man sprawled out in a position that didn't seem natural. I could hear my own heartbeat. "Stay here," I said calmly.

"Just don't scream. I hate it when people scream," Detective Black said. "And don't touch anything."

I slowly moved forward, my eyes scanning the floor as I walked closer, in case I'd step on any clues. It was pointless to pretend that this wasn't what I thought it would be. There was something sticking out of the man's chest, and soon his copper hair was clearly visible, as well as his face. Carl Scranton. Dead as dead can be.

I bent forward to observe the fountain pen lodged in his chest, where his heart would be, but there was also blood around his head. A lot of blood. I felt nauseous. Why hadn't

I had a hearty breakfast like usual? Then again, perhaps I'd be throwing that up right about now.

"What are y—oh good heavens!" Eleanor shrieked. "Is he...?"

"Call Alistair, tell him there's been a murder," I said.

ALISTAIR DIDN'T LOOK happy when he saw me. Probably because we'd interrupted his therapy session, but also because this was the second time that I'd found a dead body. I wasn't too thrilled about it either. In fact, I'd hoped that the first time would be the last time. But fate had other plans, and so here we were.

After a short while the CSI team, whose job it was to gather forensic evidence, arrived. It was getting crowded, and we were asked to step outside. Alistair and his partner, DC Daniels, soon joined us for questioning.

Despite the fact that it was getting hotter and hotter, I didn't register the warmth. After Alistair said the standard sympathetic things, he asked us to relay what had happened.

Olivia explained how we all went to get the cakes and got to the church.

"Poppy saw him first," I said. My voice didn't quite sound like mine.

Poppy held up a proud finger. "Yes, I have the eyes of a Great Tit. I spotted him immediately."

DC Daniels went red behind Alistair, and Alistair pressed his lips together, as if holding in a laugh.

"It's hawk or eagle," murmured Olivia, but Poppy went on.

"I wondered if it was part of the festival, for some reason. I asked Maggie, and she went to check it out."

Now all eyes were on me. "I did. I moved closer, carefully, just in case there was evidence on the aisle."

"Why did you consider that?" Alistair asked.

"The way he was lying there. It didn't look natural. Then I saw the pen st—sticking out of his chest." I began to feel shaky. "When I got closer, I mean—there was just so much blood spread out from under his head."

"Are you okay? You look very pale." Alistair sounded worried. He stopped scribbling in his notebook and put it away.

"I'm fine," I said, but just then black spots danced in front of my eyes. I bent forward and groaned.

The ladies made high-pitched noises of concern, and I felt many hands on my back and arms. "Perhaps we should get you into the house, let's go," Eleanor said.

"Why don't I carry her? Eleanor, if you could get the door. DC Daniels, check how the crime scene manager is getting on." Alistair slipped his arms around me and pulled me up, grunting in the effort.

"Thanks," I muttered with my eyes still closed. I hadn't lost consciousness, but the spots hadn't disappeared.

"Shut up," he said softly. "I told you you're perfect."

I couldn't help but smile.

He moved slowly—since I wasn't made of air, unlike crackers—but he carried me inside. Eleanor's home was cool, and my vision improved. "I'm okay," I said and looked up at Alistair. His lovely woody scent registered, and he looked at me with concern.

"Are you sure?" he asked.

"You can put me down." I liked being in his arms, but I had my pride.

He gently put me down and still had his arms around me after I stood up straight. "Are you sure you're okay?"

"I am." I touched his chest, before moving away. "Thanks."

The women had gathered in the kitchen. Olivia had immediately grabbed a slice of cake, while Eleanor got me a fresh glass of apple juice. They set it down in front of me at the same time.

"Thank you." I sat down and took a few sips.

Poppy eyed the cake.

"Would you like some as well, Poppy?" Eleanor asked, a smile tugging at the corners of her lips.

"Oh, yes, please. If you don't mind." She beamed. Her appetite would not be affected by something as silly as murder.

Eleanor got up again to fetch the entire cake. She put plates down for everyone. "I was saving it for the next few days, but we all desperately need this, don't we, girls? I'll bake another one tonight."

Ava and Olivia stood against the counter of the cosy kitchen while Lily sat on my other side, opposite of Poppy. Alistair was still behind me.

Phoebe and Jessica were by Muffin's basket. Muffin purred as they petted him, his tail sweeping from left to right.

"Did you see anybody leave the church as you came up?" Alistair asked.

"He was already dead for a while," I said.

"Why do you say that?"

I made a face. "I was afraid you'd ask that."

"Sorry," he said.

"The blood had dried. It hadn't just happened."

"And did you find a phone near him?"

"No," I said. "Did you not find his on him?" I asked.

Alistair shook his head.

Eleanor sighed. "In all these years—" her voice trailed off. "The church is always open. We do that in case someone wants to visit it. We had one parishioner who had insomnia and frequented the church late at night. He's passed on now, but we have always kept it unlocked just in case."

"So anyone could have entered the church?"

"Anyone," Eleanor said. "I'm just glad our house doesn't connect to the church. It used to, but we had that door sealed." She shook her head. "For something so heinous to be committed in a church. Our church." She sounded heartbroken.

"I'm sorry, Eleanor," I said, and she managed a feeble smile.

"You know, that woman, Rachel, she promised us that he'd get what he deserved. Perhaps what he deserved, in her eyes, was murder," I said as I turned to Alistair.

He simply nodded at me. Then he continued to ask basic questions about how we knew the victim, but he knew as much as we did. Soon we were free to go.

"Are you sure you're feeling better?" Alistair asked as he put a hand on my back. Eleanor was seeing the other women out.

"Yes." I smiled at him. "I promise."

He bit his lip as if he was contemplating something, then bent down and kissed my forehead. He smiled shyly and then left.

I sighed as my heart was on fire just a tiny bit.

"Yeah, right. I better call the fire department," Detective Black said.

I stuck out my tongue at him.

Eleanor returned. "Are you okay, love?"

"Yes, I just hadn't eaten much because of the cake eating contest." I groaned. "What will we do now?"

"We'll still go ahead with it."

My head shot up. "What?"

"Harold will return soon, but I'm sure he'll agree. If we cancel, then this huge shadow will be cast over this day. That is not the point of the Summer Festival. The point is to celebrate. We will simply have the eating contest somewhere else. Ava said she could arrange something with Phoebe and Jessica. They'll set something up in the village square, make sure there's shading so the pies aren't affected too much by the sun. We'll skip the tasting, though. It will take too long. We'll declare everyone a winner, and instead of winning a pie, they'll get a ribbon. Phoebe said she could get one in an hour."

"Wow, I didn't know we could be so efficient."

"Everybody can push themselves for things that matter." She patted my hand.

"Including murder."

Eleanor raised an eyebrow. "I imagine that people who do such a thing feel very strongly that it is the only option for them."

"Yes, but it is sad to think that you can erase a problem by erasing someone's life."

"Indeed," Eleanor said.

Chapter 6

By the time I returned to The Wicked Bookworm, most people had already learned that Carl had been murdered. It was hard to miss the commotion at the vicarage. A crowd had gathered, and I was sure that by now everyone knew how he was found. Gossip spread like a rash.

The bookshop was surprisingly quiet and only the Castlefield Book Club had gathered at the coffee/tea nook, except for Nancy and Olivia. Eleanor was still at the vicarage, waiting for Harold to return.

Eddie was by the counter with Sophia, who was very quiet, and Christina was the one who first spotted me. She came over and clasped my hands.

"Are you okay? They said you found that unpleasant man?" There was a line between her eyebrows as she observed me.

I hugged her. "I'm just shocked, that's all. I really don't want to make finding bodies a thing."

"You handled it well," Detective Black said.

"I understand completely. Once I found a dead badger, and I cried for days. Granted, I was ten, but still." She made a face. "Sorry, that's hardly the same, is it?"

I squeezed her hand. "Don't worry, I appreciate it."

"Was Alistair there?" she asked. She tried to sound casual, but I picked up on the slight difference in her tone.

"Yes. It wasn't what you thought. Don't worry, okay? He'll come and talk to you later."

Her eyes widened. "He will?"

I wanted to say more, but Sophia had spotted me and came over. "Maggie, Eddie told me about Carl. How dreadful. How are you holding up?"

"I'm shaken, but not stirred. Sorry, bad joke. It was just a terrible shock."

Christina excused herself and left us to chat while Eddie occasionally glanced over. He seemed to really care about Sophia.

"I hope she's not the killer then," Detective Black said. "That would be terrible."

"Yes, it certainly is. I never would have thought—anyway, I've brought your dress. Eddie put it under the counter. He also told me you're a bit of sleuth and that you solved a murder a few months ago." She looked at me expectantly.

"I did, but I prefer solving murders on paper." But then I realised that delving into this murder was the perfect excuse to spend time with Alistair without worrying about anyone's feelings, including my own. We would keep it professional.

"Still, it's very impressive. Are you going to look into this one?"

"No, of course not. There's no reason to." Except there was. A very good one. "Maybe," I added.

She smiled, though it was more of a smirk. "If you do, I'd love to help."

Three is a crowd.

"Actually, you can help."

She perked up.

"What can you tell me about him that seems important now? Like, were there fights? Rumours? Anything bad?"

She tilted her head as she contemplated this. Then she gasped. "Yes, actually. How could I have forgotten? There's a very juicy piece of information I have."

Pause.

"Well?" I asked, fighting the urge to grab her shoulders and shake it out of her.

She leaned forward. "I saw him kiss Wendy a few weeks ago. Actually, it wasn't so much a kiss as it was a make-out session," she whispered.

"Damn. But she's married to Gregor. Did he know? Did you tell him or anyone else?"

She shook her head. "No, and I don't know if he knew. I doubt it. He seemed to get along just fine with Carl."

"Okay, thank you. This is actually helpful."

"Anytime. I've got to go now. I'm sure the police will want to ask me questions as well." She was about to leave.

"Tonight, let's have dinner together. Us writers," I said. "Take your mind off the murder. My treat. We'll go to a restaurant. I'll borrow my aunt's car."

"Sure, I'll tell the others. Thanks, Maggie." She waved at Eddie and left.

"Another murder," Eddie said as I approached the counter. "I can't believe it."

"Perhaps there is no Pembroke curse, perhaps it's Castlefield that's cursed," I said.

"I hope not. I'm rather fond of our quirky village."

"Me too."

"Are you getting involved in this murder?" Eddie narrowed his eyes at me.

"Perhaps."

"Just be nice to Sophia. I like her." He turned red.

I smiled. "I'll be nice to her. Unless she's the killer."

He shook his head. "Don't joke about that. And she can't be."

"How do you know? Because she's pretty?"

"No, I mean—yes, she is pretty—but no, because we were together last night."

"You slept with her?" I said a little too loud, and the book club women in the back became very quiet all of a sudden.

"No, I did not," Eddie said loudly, then softer, "I really didn't. She wanted to watch a film with me even though it was getting late. We fell asleep on my sofa." He got red again. "So I guess we did sleep together."

I chuckled. "Don't worry, I won't tell anyone."

"You just did, remember?" He glared.

"Oops." I gave him a kiss on the cheek and then joined the women by the armchairs and coffee machine. There were also biscuits. It was a cosy nook.

"Maggie, we're going to read all of Carl's books, as well as the books by the other authors," Lily said.

"Okay," I said.

She frowned. "Don't you want to know why?"

"Because you're the local book club."

Poppy chuckled, then continued eating the biscuits.

"Alright, that's true, but no, we're going to look for clues." Lily looked proud, like a child showing their latest drawing.

"Why do you think there are clues to be found in those books?" I asked.

She sighed dramatically, which made me want to high-five her in the face. With a cactus. "None of us would have killed that man, would we? It has to be one of his writer friends. Besides, everyone knows writers are disturbed, especially when writing about murder." She raised her eyebrows defiantly.

Never mind a cactus, I'd hit her with a chair.

"Now, now, don't be jealous that Maggie's a good author. I've seen you enjoy her books, pet," Ava said.

Lily turned pale.

"Have you now?" I asked and beamed at Lily.

She grumbled something.

"But, we do believe that the other authors might be crazy psycho killers," Ava said. "So we've divided the books amongst ourselves and will try and finish them within the next few days and share our findings. Hopefully there will be clues to this latest crime." She rubbed her hands together.

"Anything we can do to help you, Maggie," Phoebe said.

So they'd already assumed I'd be looking into this. I was getting quite the reputation. Although, considering they'd asked for my help last time, perhaps I already had it.

"When is the pie eating contest?" I asked.

"It's in the village square at around three o'clock," Jessica said, stealing the last biscuit before Poppy could devour it.

"I'm not sure I'm going to go. I still feel a bit out of sorts." Besides, I had serious doubts that Alistair would join now that there was a murder case that needed solving. Not that I'd joined for him; I hadn't even known until today, but he was the only highlight at this point.

"Just think about it, lass," Ava said.

"Yes, it might be a nice distraction," Lily said.

I waited for an insult, but there was none. "Okay, thanks."

Instead of going up to my flat, I decided to pay a visit to Beth. She usually made me feel better, even if she was in one of her confused states. I regularly brought over books for her to read and did that today as well. Two new summer romance books.

Her cottage was near the vicarage, but I hoped it had all escaped her notice. I could still see his body in front of me. He wasn't a nice man; I didn't like him, but he didn't deserve to be murdered.

I let myself in with the key under the flower pot and glanced back at Alistair's cottage which was opposite Beth's. His car wasn't there. I wondered what leads he would be following, though I had a few ideas. Rachel was a good suspect, and so was the man that had punched Carl earlier. Wendy and Gregor had known him the longest, and if he was having an affair with Wendy then that made both Gregor and Wendy suspects. Carl hadn't seemed faithful to Wendy.

Beth was out in her garden with a big bottle of water and a sandwich. During the summer she was usually in better mental shape, though I wasn't sure why. She gave me a hug and invited me to sit with her. Despite my protests she got up to make me a sandwich as well, and we ate it in her garden, overlooking the small pond with dragonflies dancing above the water. Birds tweeted, and bees buzzed in the near distance. These were the nice village sounds that I missed when I was up in my flat during this time of year. I could buy a cottage, but I liked living above my shop.

Instead of talking about the murder, we only spoke about pleasant things. I was sure Beth hadn't learned of the murder yet; at least she hadn't asked me, and I was glad of that. It was an unpleasant subject, and I rather had Beth hear only nice things. When she got confused, she could mix up reality with fiction, but I also didn't want to risk her mixing someone else's reality with hers.

And so we sat in the garden, enjoying a sandwich on a hot summer's day while the bees buzzed and butterflies fluttered around, showing off their beautiful wings. Just a normal day in a normal English village.

I WAS ON MY WAY BACK to the bookshop around the time that the pie eating contest would begin. I figured I'd dash up to my flat and do some writing when someone touched my arm.

It was Alistair.

"Hi," he said.

"Hi. Aren't you working on the case?"

"We currently have that woman, Rachel—who accused Carl of plagiarism—in custody. We ruled out the guy who punched him; he has an alibi. Rachel, however, does not."

I gasped. "Did she confess?"

"No, but it's just a matter of time," he said.

"Unless she didn't do it."

Alistair grinned at me, which always did something to my insides.

Detective Black sighed.

"Do you know something?" Alistair asked.

"Of course. Hold on to your socks, you might lose them."

Alistair chuckled.

"Wendy and Carl were seen kissing by Sophia. They might have been having an affair."

He let out a low whistle. "That is good stuff. I'm impressed."

"I am Sherlock after all."

"We're about to find out," he said as he pointed in the direction of the village square. "Are you ready?"

After having talked to Beth, I actually felt like myself. It was as if finding Carl's body was a bad dream. "I shouldn't have had that sandwich," I muttered. Then added, "Yes. I'm ready."

There were six other contestants, one of whom was Stanley. He won last year.

A crowd had gathered. Christina was there, as well as Nancy. She had her camera out. She'd leave her shop for this, alright. She'd probably get a photo of me with pie all over my face printed and enlarged.

Harold had handed ribbons to all the people who had provided the pies since we had skipped the tasting. One was left for the winner of this contest. Eleanor had put napkins around our necks. She was the judge, along with Harold, and two others. "Hands behind your backs, contestants," Harold shouted. He had quite a far-reaching voice.

I stood next to Alistair, and we glanced at each other.

"Get ready. Set. Go." He blew on a whistle.

I bent forward and stuffed my face in the cherry pie. It was actually delicious, though I barely got to taste it since I was practically inhaling it. I had started in the middle and was working my way towards the edge, going around. I had no idea how fast I was. The crowd was shouting, my mouth was operating like a black hole.

Then the crowd applauded and cheered. Someone had won.

Curses. It better not be Alistair.

I finished and stood up straight, my face was covered in cherry pie and my back was sore. I looked over at Stanley who looked smug, or at least, I think he did. It was hard to tell with the apple pie all over the bottom half of his face. Then I looked at Alistair. He was still eating! Yes. I'd beat him.

He was third, but the others soon finished. The final two contestants finished at the same time.

Harold blew the whistle again, and the crowd went wild.

Alistair and I looked at each other.

"Do I have something on my face?" I said.

He laughed. "Just a tiny bit on the corner of your mouth."

I dabbed at it with my pinky. "Is it gone?"

"Oh, yes."

We both giggled.

While Harold handed out the ribbon to Stanley, I leaned over to Alistair. "I really need to start working out now. At this rate, this year's Christmas dinner will make me explode."

"I told you," he said in a low voice. "You're perfect."

Luckily my cheeks couldn't get any redder.

AFTER WE WERE HANDED wet towels to dry our faces, we were free to enjoy the rest of the day. Instead of running back inside to hide from the heat, I took a stroll towards Gus. He ran the local antique shop, but he also sold Harold's birdhouses during the Summer Festival each year. One was still there. "Sold two already, Gus?" I asked.

"People wait for them especially, you know," he said. His hair was grey, and he had a kind, round face. "I also sold the wicker baskets that Mabel made especially for the festival. When it says handmade by the locals, it sells pretty quickly."

"I can imagine. But your antique items are also very nice."

He grinned from ear to ear. "Thank you, dear. You should stop by sometime and check out what I have. Your aunt recently bought a teapot."

"Nancy did?" She always said that antique stuff was for dead people. Yet she still watched *Antiques Roadshow*.

"Err, no, no. I must have been mistaken. It was someone else." His cheeks flushed.

"Yes, because so many people wear beehives on their head," Detective Black said.

Thank goodness they didn't. One Nancy was more than enough.

I smiled at him. "No worries."

He looked relieved when someone else showed up to browse his stuff.

I continued to walk around for a bit when Alistair appeared at my side. He pressed his lips together.

"What's wrong?" I asked.

"Nothing, nothing. I just had a chat with Christina."

I glanced in the direction of my shop and just caught a glimpse of her as she disappeared behind a van that was parked in the street. "And? Did it go well?"

"Yes, I think so. She seemed relieved. Like it made sense. I think I managed to articulate what I wanted to say." He still looked like he was constipated.

"Isn't that good?"

"Yes. I feel better."

"Then why do you look like you have to go to the bathroom?"

He smirked. "Probably because I just had a difficult conversation. And maybe because I have to call you Sherlock now."

"From now until the end of time. And beyond."

He cleared his throat. "DC Daniels called earlier. He had a little accident."

Someone bumped into me and Alistair pulled me along to a quiet spot under an oak tree. Twenty paces farther and we'd be in the woods.

"Is it serious?"

"No, he'll be fine. I'm still not sure how he managed to do it. He was on the toilet...anyway, I'll be working this case alone, and I could use the help of a certain Sherlock."

"Don't you think Rachel did it?"

"She might not ever confess, and the Wendy thing is worth looking into."

"Will I get paid?" I said with a smile.

"What would you like to get paid in?"

Kisses. "Biscuits."

"Deal."

We shook hands.

Chapter 7

Christina kept herself busy in the bookshop, so I figured she didn't want to talk about Alistair. She probably needed to process it all. I went upstairs to write for a bit and after that I wanted to check out the library at the Pembroke. First, I stopped at Nancy's shop. Three customers were browsing, but they couldn't overhear us.

Nancy was flipping through a magazine at the counter. "Hi, love," she said without looking up.

"How are you liking that antique kettle you bought?" I asked.

"It was a teapot, act—" She gasped. "No, I didn't. I mean, I didn't buy anything. How dare you accuse me?"

I bit my lip to keep from laughing. "Accuse you of what, my dear aunt?"

"Oh, you little—you're too smart for your own good. Just leave it alone, will you?"

"Do you guys spoon? Which one is the big spoon and which one the little? Do you hold hands? Has he cooked you dinner? Have you had Eskimo kisses? Do you have nicknames? Does he call you Schmoopy?"

"You horrid girl, get out," she said as she started rolling up her magazine.

I shrieked and laughed as I ran out of her shop. Outside I held up my hands in the shape of a heart, but she bolted after me. I ran away giggling. She wouldn't leave her shop unattended, so I was safe.

As I neared the Pembroke, still grinning, a girl shouted my full name. She had been sitting on a bench, eating an ice cream and ran over. She had an expensive-looking handbag on her arm, and I hadn't noticed the purple streak in her dark hair earlier. Probably because I was trying to stop Nancy from killing her.

"Emblyn, right?" I said, and started strolling as she joined me.

"As you can see, my dad didn't kill me. Yay," she said dryly.

"That is a good thing. Besides, I'm sure he loves you."

"Then you're the only one of us who is," she said. "Anyways, I heard you found a dead body. What was it like?"

"Not at all fun, in case that's what you're thinking. This is the second time I've found one."

Her eyes widened. "Are you for real?"

"Yeah. How long have you lived here? You must have heard the gossip," I said.

"We moved here two weeks ago. My dad desperately wanted to move to an idyllic village now that he's getting older. It was his dream, not mine. But it didn't stop him from yanking me away from all my friends and, you know, civilisation. So here I am, in the middle of nowhere." She grunted.

"Yes, it must be terrible to be surrounded by thatched cottages, beautiful forests, and green paddocks with fluffy sheep." I conveniently left out the homicidal chicken roaming around here.

"You sound like my dad. Hate to break it to you, but this is not a great place for a fifteen-year-old."

I gasped. "Yes, it is. When I was fifteen, I had a great time here. You just have to know your way around this place."

She cocked an eyebrow. "Meaning?"

"Eddie and I used to hang out at the cemetery."

"Oh, so you had an early interest in dead bodies?" She smirked.

"No," I said and glared at her.

"Well—" Detective Black said.

"And we used to chase Mr Brooks' sheep. Or play pranks on Mr Brooks. He was very moody. Once we painted his sheep to make it look like they wore tuxedos. It was harder than we thought. He was also furious, and we never dared to tell anyone we had done it."

"How do you know I won't tell him now?" Emblyn asked with a wicked grin.

"You could try, but I'll be very impressed if you can talk to the dead."

"Oh. Good thing I wasn't planning on telling him then." She paused. "Do you think your aunt will forgive me one day?"

"One day. Eventually. I think." I glanced at her, and seeing her worried expression, added, "Just show her how great you are, and try to do something to make it up to her. She prefers action over words."

She nodded. "I'll remember that. It was really stupid of me. I don't know why I did it."

"Sometimes we do things to get noticed," I said carefully.

She looked up and pressed her lips together. "That obvious, huh? I suppose I'm quite the cliché. Spoiled rich kid with daddy issues."

"Don't worry about what it looks like. You can't help what you're feeling. But just because your dad works a lot, doesn't mean he doesn't care. Maybe village life will rub off on him, and he'll gradually spend more time with you. You could invite him to the Summer Festival. There is a wine tasting in a few days; he might like that."

"He does love wine. He's quite a wine snob."

"Then you should suggest it," I said. We had reached the bottom of the hill of the Pembroke estate.

"Good idea." She smiled, and her whole face lit up.

"You know, my aunt always complains that she can never find good help, but I know for a fact that she's not even looking. She has control issues. But maybe if you offer a trial run working at her shop, where she can let you go any second she's not happy with you, you might find her willing to give you a chance. You might end up with a job, as well as redemption." I winked at her.

"Her shop is cool, and it would give me something to do."

"And you'll meet new people."

"You are full of good ideas today, Maggie Matthews," she said.

"Those days are rare."

She sniggered. "I'll consider it. Take care."

"Bye."

She went off in the other direction, probably to check out the village square, while I went up the hill with feelings of trepidation. I hadn't been back here since I got locked up with Alistair. I realised it was just an estate, it was unlikely to be truly cursed, but I certainly had unpleasant memories associated with it.

I let myself in with the key and looked around. Everything was quiet but looked the same. On the opposite side of the broad staircase that coiled upwards was the reception desk, now empty. I went through the archway on the right side of the staircase and into the reception area. It used to have a few sofas and further in the back there had been more seats, and a small bar. Now there was a hard-wooden floor instead of a carpet, and there were a sofa and two armchairs in front of the fireplace. There also used to be a bookcase that could open to a deathtrap, but it had been sealed. All the way in the back were a piano and a dining room table with chairs.

I shivered and went up the stairs to the first floor where the library was. It had high bookcases that covered the walls and more bookcases were stacked throughout the room. There was a small wooden table in the far back. It would certainly make a grand study with some minor changes.

Miles, or someone, had already put out moving boxes and markers. I actually knew someone who collected old books, so the first box I labelled 'old books,' a second one 'bookshop,' and a third 'donate.' That would be a great start. My hands were itching. I was bound to find something valuable, although I wouldn't be able to appraise it. I started with one of the bookcases nearest to the table with the books on the bottom row, working my way up.

I wasn't sure how long it had taken me, but by the time I had cleared out four rows, Miles' cheerful greeting interrupted me.

"Hey, Miles," I said. "What are you doing here?" It couldn't be that late.

"I was actually running some work-related errands, despite the fact that my two-week holiday started on Monday. I was going to grab a drink in the pub for the first time, but Kelly told me you were here."

I took a moment to sit down; I had worked up a sweat. It didn't help that this room wasn't air conditioned. "I didn't notice anyone here."

"She saw you working diligently and didn't want to disturb."

"And she's your assistant or something? Alistair mentioned her name and that she did your shopping, I think."

Miles leaned against the nearest bookcase. "Yes. I usually don't have time for shopping, so that's what she does."

"What about the cooking then?"

"I love to cook. She knows better than to do that for me. She has two weeks off now as well. I suppose it will just be me in this massive place."

"And me." I smiled. "Not just for the books. I can always stop by, if you want." Now that I'd gotten used to Christina, I realised how nice it was to live with someone.

He leaned forward. "You're a dear. Speaking of hanging out, I would like it if you had dinner with me."

I raised my eyebrows. "Why are you saying it like that?"

"Like what?"

"Like there's a catch."

"Well, the dinner is with my father."

"Oh. That isn't too bad, is it?"

"You haven't met my father," he grumbled.

"But I will. I'd love to have dinner with you guys." I smiled.

"Great. So you're in. Great."

I narrowed my eyes at him. "There's another catch, isn't there?"

"You have to pretend to be my girlfriend." He shrugged and gave me an innocent smile.

"What? Why? We're not in a romantic comedy. Can't you just tell him you're single?"

"No. He's always pressuring me to get married, and he knows plenty of women to introduce me to. Since I turned thirty he's been even more relentless. He said he was going to set me up, whether I liked it or not, and I told him I was seeing someone." He held out his hands as if to say 'oops.'

I sighed. "Your dad must be very forceful, then."

"He's an ass. We don't get along, but I would like to get this over with. If I have to pretend to have a girlfriend for one night, so be it."

"That is, if your girlfriend agrees." I folded my arms in front of my chest.

"Make sure you get paid," Detective Black whispered in my ear.

"What's in it for me?" I said.

"What do you want?"

"I'll think about that," I said, because the only thing I could come up with on the spot was a pony. And where would I keep it?

"So you'll do it?"

"Yeah, I'll do it. It kind of sounds like fun."

"You wouldn't say that if you knew my father."

"You turned out okay, at least."

"Yes, it's a miracle. Now, speaking of dinner, would you like me to cook you some?"

My mouth began to water, despite the fact that I'd just absorbed an entire pie. "I'm actually having dinner with the other authors."

"Interesting. Let's have a drink instead, then."

I followed him down to the kitchen.

"This kitchen is small for a hotel kitchen," I said as I looked around.

"That kitchen is on the other side of this hotel. This is the one for personal use. It's quite charming, isn't it?"

I nodded. "You mentioned your dad, but where is your mother?"

"Oh, she'll also be at the dinner. She's nice, contrary to my dad."

"You really don't like him."

"No, but we won't dive into that depressing topic. How's your relationship with your parents?"

I laughed. And then elaborated since he wasn't in my head and couldn't know that was funny. "Just as dramatic, I'm afraid. My mother has mental problems, and my dad couldn't deal with it. He left me with my aunt Nancy. It was only supposed to be temporary, but he started a new family and stopped visiting frequently."

"I'm sorry to hear that."

"It's okay. We can't choose who we are born to."

He took a swig of white wine. "That is very true."

"So do you like being back here?" I asked. "Have you made friends with Pandora yet?" The first time he'd met her, she'd gone straight for his ankles.

"Ugh. Foul beast." He made a face. "But apart from the winged demon, it is lovely being back. It still has that same feel, though I have changed, of course. So has Alistair. Not in a bad way, mind. We've just grown up."

"Yeah, that's why I'm glad I didn't do it."

"Do what?"

"Grow up. I just refused."

He laughed. It was a nice change from that fake, but charming smile. "You're not who I thought you would be when I first met you."

"When you first met me I was being interviewed by the police about a murder."

"Yes. That's probably why. Speaking of murder...are you getting involved in this one? You have quite the reputation as a problem-solver. When Eleanor brought me cake after I moved in, she told me all about your shenanigans. And the fact that a lot of people think you can solve their problems. Did someone once ask you to find her rooster?"

"Ah, yes. That's right. A woman named Sylvia asked me that. He was a special rooster, and she claimed he could tell the future."

Miles laughed.

"He couldn't, but one of the residents, who had a gambling problem, stole the rooster, so he could make a fortune betting."

"Did he?"

"No. The rooster was not psychic, but either way, I brought the rooster back. This was years ago. The rooster is long gone now. There are still people who believe he was psychic."

"Right. And the reason you felt the need to accept Sylvia's proposition was because...?"

"I like helping people. And I like mysteries. Easy choice. Besides, you can't judge me. You just asked me for help yourself."

He took a moment to think about this. "I'm afraid you're right. Oh, well, live and learn."

I smiled and shook my head.

We finished our drinks and then he walked me to the front door. I already had two boxes full, and he said he'd take care of them. The dinner date with his parents was this Friday, and when he said it like that, I got nervous. I really was going to meet his parents. And pretend to be his girlfriend. Then again, it would probably be good experience for a novel. *I think.*

Halfway to my bookshop, I bumped into someone. She was staring at the ground, and when her eyes met mine, she started crying. It was Rachel.

I put my hand on her arm and made soothing sounds. I waited for her to calm down. So far the noises she made could only be understood by dogs.

She sniffed a few times and took a deep breath. "The p—police just let me go." She let out another sob. "They had no evidence, but they said I couldn't leave. They think I did it. Me. Can you believe it? I've had mice in my attic for years because I didn't want to kill them. Do they honestly think I would bash someone's skull in?"

I gasped. "Cause of death was blunt force trauma?"

She looked at me as if *I'd* hit my head.

"Sorry, yes, no. Terrible. Terrible of them."

"Exactly. I wouldn't hurt a fly." Then she smacked her arm. "Blasted mosquitoes," she murmured. "Anyway, I know it has nothing to do with you, but I just had to vent. Do you believe

I killed him?" She took an eager step closer, her brown eyes searching mine.

"I simply don't know. I'm keeping my options open," I said. And it was the wrong thing to say, because she started crying again.

This was becoming a very long day.

"It was a very short one for Carl Scranton," Detective Black said.

Chapter 8

I arrived at the B&B still mulling over my conversation with Rachel. She seemed very distraught at the idea that she was murder suspect number one. Of course, who wouldn't be? Was she pretending, though? Or was she genuinely scared? She'd apparently come here all alone, just to put Carl to shame. And now she was stuck in a village where everyone thought she was a murderer. That could not be easy.

"But it's not your problem, or responsibility," Detective Black said.

"I know that. I never said it was. I just—feel for her." I sighed and rang the bell.

Mrs Suzuki—the owner—opened the door with a smile, revealing the dimples in her cheeks. "Maggie, how nice to see you. Your colleagues said you were coming."

I laughed. I wasn't working with them, but I suppose they were the closest thing to colleagues I'd ever have.

"I'm your colleague," Detective Black said, slightly offended.

Sophia walked in. "I thought it might be you. Guys, she's here," she called to the others.

"Where are we going?"

"I'll take you somewhere nice. Follow me, I've parked out front."

Wendy stumbled into the corridor while Gregor tried to grab her. She fell against Sophia, who held her upright.

"Are you okay?" Mrs Suzuki and I asked simultaneously.

"She's fine. She's just had a few drinks already," Gregor said, with an apologetic smile. "Carl's death has affected us all."

"Some more than others," Detective Black said.

"Of course, I understand," Mrs Suzuki said. "Well, you go out and try to have fun, take your mind off things."

"Thanks, Mrs S. See you." I eyed Wendy, who had adjusted her light hair and stood up straighter. They followed me out to Nancy's green Land Rover. Sophia sat down next to me, and the married couple sat in the back.

I drove to a seafood restaurant by the sea. It looked expensive, but it wasn't too bad. I figured it would impress them and hopefully get them to open up. We had a seat by the window. The table cloth was red, and the napkins were folded into swans. Chandeliers were dotted across the ceiling, though they weren't on now. It was still light out and there were plenty of people eating outside. I hated eating outside; too many bugs around my dinner. But several double doors were opened up, so we could hear the seagulls and the rustle of the sea in the near distance.

"This looks nice," Wendy said. "And it's your treat, isn't it, Macy?"

"Wendy," Gregor hissed.

"It's Maggie, and yes, it is," I said.

"Lovely. We'll start by ordering a nice bottle of champagne," she said.

"Wendy, stop it. Just because we're struggling, doesn't mean we can leech off others when given the opportunity. Have you no pride?" Gregor said.

She pouted. "Why not? After everything that happened today." Tears welled up in her eyes.

Gregor glanced at me and Sophia. "I'm sorry about this." He actually blushed and continued to tell her off.

Poor man. All of this was made worse by the fact that his wife had been snogging Carl. I would just have to find out if it was a once-off or if they were having an affair.

"Just be subtle. As long as they don't feel like you're questioning them, it should be fine," Detective Black said.

After Gregor was done berating his wife, she grabbed the menu and held it in front of her face, purposely ignoring her husband.

"Lovely marriage. An inspirational couple," Detective Black said dryly.

Sophia and I exchanged a glance.

"I'm sorry for your loss," I said to Gregor and Wendy's menu. "I didn't get a chance to say that earlier. Were you close?"

Gregor answered. "We were friends, yes. We've known each other a few years now. I just didn't expect this at all. He doesn't know anybody here. Not that I know of."

"He was...talking to a lot of women," I said.

At this Wendy lowered her menu and glared at me. "So what? Can't he talk to people? Make friends? Is that a crime punishable by death?"

"No, not all, but something in his life must have led to this murder. Whether it was simply a case of being in the wrong place at the wrong time or not."

A waitress appeared at our table. Wendy ordered a bottle of wine and lobster. It was the most expensive meal on the menu, but that was fine by me. I reassured Gregor that he could choose whatever he liked as well. He still chose a simple fish and chips, while Sophia ordered something with scallops. I also chose the fish and chips, because I wasn't too big on seafood. The only reason I'd come here was because I wanted to get them to loosen up their tongues.

We chatted about writing and our favourite books, while I made sure their wine glasses were being refilled. This meal was going to cost me, but hopefully it would generate clues and then it would be worth it.

I missed Alistair. It would have been nice to have a fellow, non-imaginary sleuth at this table, but I was glad to get to know Sophia a bit. If Eddie really liked her, which he did, then I wanted to get to know her better. And hope she didn't turn out to be a murderer.

It was easy enough to work out that financially speaking, Wendy and Gregor weren't doing too well, but they had a serious passion for writing and both seemed to have admired Carl. Sophia was new to the group and made it clear she was eager to learn from all of them, and she even came across as self-conscious when it came to her writing career.

"So, what did you guys think of that woman, Rachel, who accused Carl of stealing her work?" I asked as we'd moved on to dessert. I had skipped it; the pie I'd devoured earlier was enough dessert for the day.

"Rubbish," Wendy said, with her mouth full of ice cream.

"I agree." Gregor leaned forward. "Carl was a visionary. A craftsman. He wouldn't have done that. He had integrity."

Are you sure about that? I glanced at Sophia who pretended to be fascinated by her tiramisu.

It was very tempting to mention the kiss that Sophia had witnessed, but I didn't want to out her; they were still part of the same writing group. I would have to talk to them tomorrow with Alistair present. It would be easier to force them to talk when one of us had a shiny badge.

Clearly both of them had rose-coloured glasses on when it came to Carl. I didn't believe it, though. And not because he'd flirt with a pineapple if it had boobs, but because he hadn't seemed surprised when he saw Rachel.

"We were actually working on a project together," Wendy said. "We were brainstorming about a novel, but then all of a sudden he said he wanted me to write it, because he had an idea he wanted to pursue. If he was a thief, then he wouldn't have done that, would he? He would not have helped me brainstorm, but then turn around and work on his own novel."

If it was his own novel. Perhaps he had stolen another piece of work. Maybe that's why Rachel was here. It could be that he'd done it again, and she killed him. It could be that he was planning on stealing the work from Wendy, and she was lying.

Too many ifs.

"That's a good point," I said. "Do you guys know where he was staying?"

"At the Pembroke," Gregor said.

"No. It's not a hotel right now, despite what the sign says."

"What's that supposed to mean?" Wendy asked. She could barely keep her eyes open and her words were slurring.

Gregor played with his napkin.

He knew. He knew where he had been staying.

"Interesting," Detective Black said.

"Do you think he knew someone here?" Sophia asked.

"Maybe," I said. For now there was another question I would have to ask Gregor tomorrow.

"I think I need another bottle of wine," Wendy said.

"Cheque, please," I shouted.

AFTER I HAD RECOVERED from the initial shock the receipt had given me, I drove the others back to the local B&B. Gregor helped his wife to the door, though she insisted that she was fine. She nearly fell into the nearby potted plant.

"Thanks for dinner," Sophia said.

I switched off the engine. "You're welcome. Will you be okay?"

"I will. It's just very weird that this happened. I hope we can go home soon. That police detective said we couldn't leave. I don't mind, though. I like Eddie."

"He's a good guy and my best friend. Be good to him, please." Otherwise I'd have to sic Pandora on her.

"Do you really think you'll solve this murder?" she asked.

"I'll try."

She got out of the car and said goodbye before slamming the car door shut.

I took a moment to gather my thoughts and then drove back home where I parked Nancy's car in front of our shops. It was dark by now but not chilly. I took a stroll to Alistair's cottage where the lights were on.

What would he be up to? It had to be strange for him to live on his own when he'd been living with Christina. Was he lonely?

I rang the doorbell and waited.

He opened the door in a shirt and jeans. It was the most casually dressed I'd ever seen him in.

"Hi," I said.

"Hey, what are you doing here? Not that I'm not happy to see you. Come in." He led me to his back garden where he had been sitting, drinking red wine and...knitting.

"You're knitting?" I gasped.

He put his hands in his pockets and avoided eye contact. "Hugh—DC Daniels—got me involved. It's relaxing."

"I'm not judging you," I said and chuckled. "It's actually very cool."

"Yeah, right."

"No, it is. In fact, I've always wanted to learn. Maybe you can teach me."

He looked up at me. "Really? I wouldn't mind."

"Good. Now get me a nice cool glass of water, and we'll talk murder."

He grinned. "As you wish, milady."

I sat down and studied his handiwork. It looked like he was making a scarf. It was coming along nicely. Especially for a beginner. He hadn't dropped a stitch yet.

He returned and put a glass of water in front of me. "So what have you discovered?" He moved his knitting out of the way and sat down next to me, leaning forward. I could smell his aftershave.

I told him about the dinner and what I picked up from Gregor.

"You think he knew where Carl was staying? Why wouldn't he just say?"

"Perhaps he wants to protect his reputation. They all thought very highly of him, even Sophia seemed to respect him as a writer."

Alistair raised his eyebrows. "I'll guess we'll go talk to Gregor and Wendy tomorrow."

"I look forward to it, partner."

He smiled warmly. "Me too."

Detective Black rolled his eyes.

"Isn't that kids' scavenger hunt Saturday?" I asked.

"Yes. I'm in charge of the clues and everything. The main prize is a treasure with a bunch of fake coins and jewels. They look very real, though. The kids will love it."

"And how are the clues coming along?"

"Fine. I think. They end up in riddles, but I'm not the best at rhyming. In one riddle I rhyme 'horse' with 'four', it's terrible." He made a face as if he tasted something sour.

"I had some inspiration a few days ago and came up with some riddles and ideas for where to hide things in the woods. And what. I never told you, because, well, I didn't think Christina wanted me to talk to you, but now that you've talked about things, maybe I can help. If you want my help, that is. I don't want to step on your toes."

"Now you say that. What about the last murder investigation where you basically took over from the start?"

"That was because the Castlefield Book Club had asked me, and I didn't want to let them down." I had also wanted to impress him.

"Sure, sure. But no, I won't be offended. I just want the kids to have a good time," he said.

I stayed for an hour longer while we went over ideas for the treasure hunt. I'd email him my clues later, but for now we had a solid plan. He walked me to the door when it was time to leave, and we hugged.

Things were all delightfully normal. We were becoming friends.

SNOWBALL HAD BEEN FED, and I let her out of the cage so she could roam around. Usually she hopped about the room before lying down near the fireplace. She was a very chill bunny.

Christina came in just as I'd settled in on the sofa. I was in the mood to just sit and relax without the TV on.

"Maggie, can we talk?" she said. Her voice was strained.

"Yes, of course." I sat up straighter. "Are you okay?"

"Did anything happen between you and Alistair while he and I were still together?" she asked.

I swallowed. The question I'd been dreading.

"It's probably too late to fake your death and move," Detective Black said.

"I didn't know he had a girlfriend at that time, but there was a moment where we almost kissed." My heart was racing. I was so happy I'd made a new friend; Christina was wonderful. Now it was very likely I would lose that friend.

"Who stopped the almost-kiss?"

I felt my cheeks warm. "Err, we were distracted by a noise."

"So, if not for that noise, you would have kissed?"

I closed my eyes briefly. "Yes, I think so."

"And he never told you he had a girlfriend?" she asked.

"No. Sorry."

She paused. "Do you have feelings for him?"

Crap. I couldn't lie to her, but I didn't want to say it out loud. That made it real. "I have—I mean, yes, I think I—I do."

"That's what I thought." She shook her head. "Seeing you guys at that pie eating contest, the way he was looking at you. Not to mention that he would have never done something like that, not while I was with him. I think he only joined that contest because you were in it."

"He didn't know I was in it until today."

She shook her head and smiled wryly. "No, I overheard him. He was talking to Eleanor about the festival a while back. She was trying to get him to join the pie eating contest, but he vehemently declined the offer. That is, until she mentioned that you had joined."

I felt like she'd just tied a ribbon around my heart and pulled it. "Really?"

"Are you really surprised?" Detective Black asked. "You do have functioning eyes, don't you?"

"He told me some things today that helped me get closure, but he also told me there was someone in the village he had feelings for. I didn't have to ask who he fancied, because I'd seen it during the contest." Christina didn't look upset, but instead there was something distant and cool about her.

"Are you angry with me? For not telling you?" I asked. "I didn't do it to hurt you, but I had downplayed it in my head. I even thought I'd imagined certain things. I mean—" I glanced at Detective Black, "I have a big imagination. Denial also played a role. Like, a lot of denial. I pretty much ate it for breakfast. Eggs, toast, and a side dish of pure denial." *Someone please stop me.*

"I'm not angry. I'm disappointed."

Two words that hit me in the chest like a hammer. It was way worse than her being angry.

"Most of all, I feel very stupid."

"No, no, you're not—" I started.

She held up a hand. "I just need some time." Then she got up and went to her room.

I groaned and slid off the sofa to lie on the floor, face down. Snowball came over and sniffed my ear.

Things had been so much easier when I'd stay in my office and only made friends with fictional people.

Chapter 9

That Thursday morning was another hot start to the day. I wore a white shirt and shorts, bringing along my pocket knife. I didn't feel like carrying a handbag, but luckily my phone fitted in my back pocket. Christina had breakfast in her room, and I hadn't seen much of her. She needed some time, and I would give it to her. I completely understood and wouldn't pressure her. But I missed her.

Alistair was waiting downstairs, browsing the crime section.

"Are you going to buy a book? You haven't done that since you've moved back." My eyes twinkled as I contemplated all the great books I could recommend to him.

"I don't know. Most of the time my head is too busy to read," he said as he scanned my outfit. "You look nice."

"Thanks." Thank goodness the air conditioning was on. "But reading is relaxing."

He shrugged. "I'd rather do something physical."

"Like knitting?" I tried not to smile.

"Are you mocking me?" He leaned forward. "That's very brave, don't you think?"

"I'm not afraid of you," I said as I crossed my arms and did my best to give him an intimidating stare.

He smiled slowly and was about to say something when someone cleared their throat. We looked up at Christina.

"Eddie called to see if I could cover for him. He wants to take Sophia out. I said I would, so I'll start right now," she said, maintaining eye contact with only me.

"Oh, yes. Of course, thank you." I checked out the counter where Brian was helping a few customers. We'd only just opened, so it wasn't terribly busy.

I glanced at Alistair, who was staring after her. "I thought I'd cleared the air with her. I guess she's still upset," he said.

"She is upset, but with me."

"What? Why?"

"I'll tell you while we head over to the B&B. Come on."

Outside the temperature was steadily rising, despite the fact that it was still morning. This time I had remembered to put sunscreen on, but I still wished I was a vampire so I had a good excuse not to go out when the sun was shining. I much preferred autumn, or winter, where I could snuggle up in warm blankets and wear warm layers of clothing to protect me from the cold. There was no escaping the heat, though. It was everywhere.

As we passed Nancy's shop, a woman ran out, crashing into Alistair. She clutched his arms. "She's mad, I tell you. Mad!"

Nancy came out with a dustpan and held it over her head. She was dressed in all black and wore less makeup than usual. Her skin also looked blotchy under her eyes. Had she been crying? She rarely did that. I was fairly certain that if she broke both her wrists, she'd barely twitch an eyebrow.

The woman dove behind Alistair. She was probably a tourist, otherwise Nancy's behaviour would not have been a surprise. Also, Nancy would never hit anyone hard. She just enjoyed chasing people off with household objects.

"Miss Knightley," Alistair said stiffly. "What do you think you're doing?"

"She—she implied I was fat."

"I didn't," the woman shrieked. "I simply said that her black outfit looked nice on her. It's slimming."

Nancy growled like a rabid dog and advanced. I stepped in front of Alistair, who was still guarding the woman, though quite possibly against his will since she was firmly clutching his shoulders.

"Nance, I'm sure she didn't mean it that way. Let's go inside for a bit. It's cooler there. Come on." I nudged her back into her shop. Alistair came in a moment later, having sent the terrified woman off.

"What's going on?" I asked, after she'd plopped down on a barstool behind the counter.

"Nothing. I just—you see, I've been dating someone," she said, as if it was a big reveal.

"Oh, no. Really? What a surprise," I said dryly.

"Yes, exactly. I know it may come as a shock that I'm a desirable woman, but I am." She looked pointedly at Alistair.

He blushed.

"But yes, I have found romance, and it has found me. Except that it was short-lived."

Alistair frowned. "Meaning?"

"She got dumped," I said.

Nancy reached for the dust pan on the counter, and Alistair pulled me back. "Okay, now. Calm down. I'm sorry to hear that. Have you been dating long?"

She looked at me. "About four months."

"Wow. Why didn't you tell me sooner?" I asked. "You know I would have been nothing but happy for you."

"It's just—we wanted to see where it went, first. Also, we were enjoying the fact that nobody had opinions on it, or was gossiping about us. You know how it can be."

"But it's me," I said. "Do you remember that time you went skinny dipping with friends and returned with a poison oak rash on your bum? Who was the one who put ointment on it?"

She frowned. "I did."

"I know, but I would have done it if you'd asked me, so there." I folded my arms.

"What do you want? A medal?"

"No, I want you to share things that go on in your life," I said.

"Alright, I suppose I could have told you sooner."

I leaned forward. "What was that?"

"I'm sorry, you wretched child. *I'm sorry*. But now he's dumped me, as you so eloquently put it. It doesn't matter."

"Did he say why?" Alistair asked.

"No. Not at all. I might have to curse him."

Alistair chuckled, but she glared at him, shutting him up immediately.

"Perhaps you should go and talk to Gus," I said.

She shook her head. Her sculpted hair in the shape of a beehive didn't move at all. "No, it's fine. I can handle myself. Revenge is a dish best served cackling maniacally."

"Well, if we can do anything—" Alistair started.

"You're a dear, so you are." She pinched his cheek. "Say, now that you're single, how about you give Maggie a go?"

"Nancy," I growled and stole a glance at Alistair who must have been equally embarrassed, but he just smiled.

"You never know what the future holds," he said, then grabbed my arm. "Come on, we've got a murder to solve. Feel better soon, Miss Knightley."

"Call me Nancy," she said after a brief moment of hesitation just as we exited the shop.

"Did you hear that? That means she likes you," I said to Alistair.

He switched positions with me so that I'd be covered by the shade, while he was partially in the sun. "What's not to like?" he said, "I know how to knit."

I TOLD ALISTAIR WHAT had happened between Christina and me on the way to the B&B.

"I'll talk to her," he said.

"No, you won't. You already had your conversation with her; that was between you and her. But what we discussed, that was between us. Don't worry."

"How can I not? You guys are good friends, and I don't want to be the reason that it's ruined. This is my fault."

"It's human to talk about fault and blame when someone's been hurt, but she would have been hurt no matter what. She'll deal with it, we'll deal with it. It's just the way it is."

"But aren't you upset?"

"Of course. But I can't force her to forgive me, nor do I want to. Hopefully, we'll get through this. If not, there isn't much that can be done. We do what we do, and the consequences can be what we want or not."

He sighed. “I just don’t want to see you get hurt.”

I smiled at him. “Pain is part of life, unfortunately. Look, have you found anything out about Carl? Anything new?”

“The pathologist should do the autopsy soon. It did look like Carl was either hit on the head or he fell and hit his head. I suspect he was hit because the benches near him didn’t have any blood on them. There was also very little blood coming from the wound in his chest. He was probably already dead when he was stabbed with that fountain pen.”

“Anything special about that pen?”

“Not that I can tell. It looked expensive, though.”

Across the street Pandora chased a couple of children, who were blowing bubbles at her and then ran away. She seemed to enjoy it since she wasn’t trying to peck their ankles or drag them back to hell. Instead she simply chased after them.

“Could the fountain pen have been part of that prize he showed off in the pub?” I asked.

“I don’t know. That’s easy enough to find out.”

“Do you think he could have been hit with that prize? The quill?”

“Yes, that thought crossed my mind. It wasn’t found near him, and since we still don’t know where he was staying, we can’t search his belongings.”

“Well, hopefully Gregor can help with that.” We arrived at the B&B.

Mrs Suzuki showed us in. Gregor and Wendy were sitting in the garden, feeding the fish in the pond. The garden was big and had several benches and tables for people to sit. The B&B had six available rooms that were quite large and popular, especially during the Summer Festival.

Wendy looked pale and Gregor was staring at the pond. We were about to make their day worse.

Alistair approached them and introduced himself. "You already know Miss Matthews."

"What is she doing here?" Wendy asked.

"She occasionally works as a police consultant," Alistair said.

I nearly exploded with joy. If I could get the police to officially recognise me as one, maybe I'd get paid. Not that I needed the money, but this sleuthing did take away from valuable writing time.

Both Wendy and Gregor now looked apprehensive.

"Perhaps, Gregor, you could start by telling us where Carl Scranton was staying. He clearly wasn't staying at the B&B, and also not at the Pembroke." Alistair sounded calm, but there was a threatening undertone that implied lying would be very bad. It was quite impressive.

"What makes you think—"

"I know you know, so unless you want his murderer to get away with it, you better tell me." Alistair took a step closer to the bench. "Do you want the murderer to get away with it?"

Gregor swallowed. "No, of course not. I just didn't want anyone to think badly of him. He's a good bloke, he just—well, he liked women. And from what I understand, he knew someone here and was staying with her. I overheard him on the phone, convincing her to let him stay with her. I don't know her name or anything. I suspect it was someone he liked, he was looking forward to staying here. He usually hated small villages, but he was excited about this." He shrugged.

"Why didn't you tell me?" Wendy asked him.

"Because he told us all that he was staying at the Pembroke, so I figured he didn't want it to come out. I was just looking out for him."

Alistair scribbled in his notebook. "Thank you, but next time try to look out for him by actually helping. We need the truth if we want to solve his murder."

Gregor looked at the ground. "Yes, I'm sorry."

"Now, if we may speak to your wife in private."

His head shot up. "Why?" He looked at her.

"You can ask me anything you like in front of my husband, Detective."

Famous last words.

"Alright then. How long had you been having an affair with Carl Scranton?"

Gregor nearly fell off the bench.

"I didn't. I don't know what you're talking about." She crossed her arms.

"Classic defensive body language. She's lying," Detective Black whispered in my ear.

"Please, don't lie to me, Miss Cohen."

She avoided eye contact with her husband and sat up straighter. "It lasted a few months, on and off. We ended things only recently."

Gregor got up and ran both hands through his long hair. It was in a ponytail, and he was messing it up. I wondered if it took long to wash. What conditioner did he use? It looked very shiny.

Focus.

"How recent?" Alistair asked.

"A week ago."

"Who ended it and why?"

"He did. And I don't know why. I suspected it had something to do with the new girl. Sophia. She was following him around like a puppy. It was clear she was after him. Maybe he decided to give her a try. Look, before you think I was heartbroken, I wasn't. We always knew it was casual and meaningless. That's why it was appealing. I wasn't looking to leave my husband."

"Just sleep with another man," Gregor filled in.

She said nothing.

"Did anybody know about the affair?"

She shook her head.

"Can you think of anyone who would want to kill him?"

Again she shook her head.

"Did you love him?" Gregor asked this time.

She nodded.

Gregor let out an angry scream that made me flinch.

"That will be all for now," Alistair said, in that same business-like tone. Despite the fact that a man's world had just come crumbling down. "Don't leave the village and don't give me another reason to come down here," he said, glaring at Gregor.

We left them to sort out the remnants of their marriage. "Will they be okay?" I asked when we were back out front.

"You mean happy and together? No. Smart enough to break up and move on? I hope so." He checked his notepad. "Wendy mentioned Sophia. Isn't Eddie quite taken with her?"

"Yes. They're actually spending the day together. We can't go and question them. Eddie will never forgive me if I interrupt their date to question her for murder. But what if Wendy was right, what if he used her and then dumped her, and she killed him."

"That's quite a leap, but yes, it is possible. It's also possible that Wendy is trying to shift the spotlight. We'll find them, and then I'll question her on my own while you stay close-by."

He really was sweet. "Thank you. Good plan."

I was still thinking about Gregor and Wendy. "Can you believe how easily Wendy spoke about being unfaithful? Like it was nothing. I mean, Gregor clearly loved her, and I think he cared deeply about Carl, for whatever reason. He must be shocked to the core."

"Yes, I suppose so."

I glanced at Alistair. "Is that all you can say?"

"Maggie, I've seen far worse than cheating spouses, trust me. And if I'd let everything get to me, I'd go mad."

The village square was busy by now and the sun was high in the sky. "Yeah, I get that. I'm just not used to it."

"Don't you write about this sort of thing?"

"Yes, but then it's different. Oh, look, there they are."

Today's event was flower arranging in the village square. Men, women, and children had joined while several volunteers walked around to help. There was Helena from the flower shop and several others. Eddie and Sophia were working on a bouquet with lots of twigs and lilies.

"You stay here," Alistair said and strode over to them.

He was pretty impressive when he was all business. And despite the fact that I had a big role to play in solving the previous murder, I had a lot to learn from him.

"And I bet you're looking forward to that," Detective Black said. "I think it's time for an intervention. I'm going to have to strap a laptop to your back. You need to write more and focus on fictional detectives instead of real ones."

But I had planned on having more of a life, and if my fictional detective was complaining, it meant that I was doing something right.

Chapter 10

I lingered near someone who was selling balloons. He had one shaped like a bunny, and I had no choice but to buy it. I tied the string around my wrist so it wouldn't float away.

Alistair had taken Sophia aside to chat with her while Eddie repeatedly glanced at them. If he was already this protective of her, I hoped she would stay here. They did make a cute couple. I prayed that her liking Carl was a lie, if only because he was so dreadful, and I liked to think she had better taste. Of course, the fact that she seemed interested in Eddie bode well.

I started walking around the square, browsing the same stalls. Gus, from the antique shop, was smiling at a customer, but as soon as he saw me, his expression turned serious, and he looked away.

I weaved my way through the crowd, which was quite large at this time, and stopped at his stall. "Hi, Gus," I said.

He looked up as if he hadn't seen me. "Oh, Maggie, how nice to see you."

There was a couple browsing, but nobody else was within earshot.

"I'm sorry to hear about you and my aunt," I said, trying to sound casual.

He turned red. "Err, yes, me too. She is quite lovely."

I inhaled slowly. It was strange to think that this friendly man had broken my aunt's heart. She wouldn't say it, she certainly wouldn't cry in front of me, but I knew, and I had to fight the urge to throw the nearest thing on the stall at him. Unfortunately, it was an old hand-embroidered linen tray cloth.

Several questions were fighting to make it to my lips, but this wasn't the time or place to ask such personal things, so I swallowed them. "Have a nice day."

He sighed, as if relieved, then wished me the same thing.

I continued on my way, wondering why he broke up with her and why he looked so guilty about it. It seemed that he felt bad, but was it because he broke up with her? Or something else?

"Perhaps some sleuthing is in order?" Detective Black suggested, but disappeared again.

Alistair met me as I neared the church.

"And?" I asked.

"She said that she had a bit of a crush on him, but it was innocent. She mostly admired his work, that was all." He checked his notebook. "She was clear that he'd never made a pass at her, and neither had she tried anything with him."

"Did you believe her?"

Alistair shrugged. "I don't know. She didn't seem surprised that I asked her."

"Perhaps because she was aware that she'd been following him around? Although she wasn't like that when they were here, not that I saw. Carl was flirting with all sorts of women, but he didn't pay much mind to his fellow writers."

"It could be that it's not related to his flirting ways at all," Alistair said.

"Yes, but that brings us back to Rachel."

"Why don't we think about it over some lunch?" he said. "My treat. And I like your balloon. It makes it easy to spot you in a crowd."

"If only the killer was easy to spot."

WE HAD LUNCH IN THE Rose where it was quiet, dark, and cool. My balloon was tied to my chair, which Alistair had pulled back for me. He had never done such a thing before, but I appreciated the gesture. Perhaps at the next lunch I'd pull out his chair. Keep him on his toes.

We ordered sandwiches with crisps and had cold drinks to further cool us off.

"If we keep Rachel out of the equation, why do you think Carl was killed in the church?" I asked.

Alistair took a sip of his ice tea. "I guess it's nice and quiet, and you can be sure you're not seen."

"But whoever he was meeting there must have known it was open, which would suggest a local."

"It could be that they tried the church doors the night before, or perhaps asked someone? I don't know. And why do you think he was meeting someone there? He could have just as easily decided to visit the church and then gotten interrupted."

We stared at each other.

"Unlikely," we said simultaneously.

"But not impossible," he added.

"Agreed."

"If only we had his phone," Alistair muttered. "That's another reason I suspect he was meeting someone. But without his phone we can't be certain. We also can't be certain if he invited the killer to meet him at the church or the other way around."

"He had been punched in the pub before. Maybe he felt like he needed to be cheered up and wanted to meet a woman there? Maybe he went a step too far, and she tried to protect herself? Or maybe she was married too, and her husband had followed her? Found them together?"

"The pen jammed into his chest suggests that it was something more, that there was some message."

"Could it have anything to do with the supposedly stolen manuscript? A pen in the chest is a pretty strong message. Especially if he was hit on the head with that award for his writing."

"Which again leads to Rachel. But we have no evidence."

"What if he's done it before? Steal, I mean. Perhaps I can dig up some rumours on the Internet, and see if I can find any other potential vict—" my voice trailed off as Callum brought our orders.

"Don't stop on my account, dearie. I know you were talking about murder, if only because most of the locals are. Actually, even the tourists are. It's quite hot news." He put down the plates and was in no hurry to leave.

"As if it isn't hot enough already," I muttered.

"So," Callum said without further ado, "are you two on a date?"

Alistair nearly spat out his ice tea.

My body turned on the heating, which wasn't very difficult since I was already hot. "No," I said and glared at him.

He just raised a perfectly plucked eyebrow and turned to Alistair. "Are you sure?"

"Oh, yes," Alistair said. "Maggie's just so...blegh. Why would I date her? She's terrible."

"Alright, there's no need for that," I said. "You're not so great yourself, you know? Your hair is too perfect, and you wear suits pretty much all the time. Do you shower in them?"

"Wouldn't you like to know?"

"Okay," Callum said. "It is a date, but a really bad one. Got it." He strolled off.

"Don't spread any rumours; it's not true." I turned to Alistair. "Great. The whole village will think we're dating by tonight."

"It will be fine, I'm sure. People will gossip anyway. Remember that time when our history teacher was sick for three weeks, and the whole village talked about how he was dying and had one foot in the grave? I'm fairly sure the funeral undertaker had started arrangements. And then he strolled in with a tan and not a care in the world."

Callum returned to bring the side salads. They had only just introduced those since they were trying to be a more healthy pub. The 'salad' consisted of three lettuce leaves and four carrots. He moved around a few things to make room for the dishes.

"That's right. He'd secretly—though quite obviously—gone on holiday. What was his excuse for having a tan again?"

"He'd been resting in the garden without sunscreen," Alistair said. "In October. When it had rained all those weeks."

Callum leaned forward. "Speaking of funeral undertakers, did you see there's a new one? He's renovating All Wood, and also changing the name."

"Thank goodness," Alistair said. "But why hasn't Mr Piper returned? Wasn't he visiting relatives abroad? Somewhere hot, I believe."

"Well, yes, I'm fairly certain it's hot where he went," Callum said as he folded his arms. Mr Piper had never been a friendly man by any means.

Alistair just stared, waiting.

"He died," I said.

"Oh." Then his eyes widened. "Ooh. No. No. No. I really thought he'd gone to visit relatives. I told his wife the other day to enjoy her time without him before he'd come back."

Callum laughed.

"It's not funny. She looked horrified."

Callum laughed louder.

I bit my lip to keep from laughing. It was very difficult. I could just picture that poor woman. Just like Mr Piper, she was quite horrid and disliked most people, animals, and inanimate objects. She had also once expressed her dislike for chocolate, flowers, and happiness. Okay, maybe not happiness, but it was clearly implied.

"Thank you, I needed that," Callum said after he was done laughing. "Now, I'll leave you to your date."

"It's not a date," I said, but he was good at pretending not to hear things.

Alistair smiled at me. "Even if this is not a date, may I ask if there's anything new going on? Apart from the murder, of course."

"I've been helping Miles with the library at the Pembroke. He said I could do whatever I wanted with the books, so it's pretty great."

"But isn't that a big library?"

"Yes."

"So won't that take a lot of time?"

"Yes."

"So you'll be there a lot."

"Yes." I smiled.

Alistair pursed his lips as he considered this. "I see."

"Do it," Detective Black said.

I leaned forward. "And I'm having dinner with him and his parents tomorrow."

Alistair's eye twitched. "What? Why?"

"They want to meet his new girlfriend," I said.

"What? You're—what?" he asked in a high voice.

I grinned. "Why? Is that weird?"

"It's—err, well, he just didn't mention it last time we spoke. I mean, since when—"

"So you guys talked about me the last time you spoke?"

"Look here, that's not the point," he said. "Since when did you two start dating?"

Though I was having fun, it was time to come clean. "We're not. He just needed to get his dad to back off and he wanted me to pretend. It's just one dinner."

"And you said yes to this?"

I shrugged. "Why not? He needed my help. I'm sure it will be interesting. And anything interesting is fuel for the writer."

ALISTAIR WALKED ME back to the bookshop before going on his way. He had been in a mood ever since I told him about the Miles thing. It made me like him more, but I had to focus on the investigation. Which, for now, was at a standstill. What I really wanted to know was where Carl had been staying and why he felt the need to lie about it.

When I walked into the bookshop, the cold air was as welcome as an ice lolly to a snowman. The shop seemed busy, but that was only because the Castlefield Book Club was there, even Olivia. At least Stanley had several employees, and his wife could take breaks when she wanted, not that she did that often. She loved working at the bakery. They all rushed over as soon as they noticed me.

Judging by the notebooks in their hands and the excited gleam in their eyes, I figured they had 'clues' to share with me. I loved them for wanting to help. They really were my favourite bunch.

"We've all reached our deadline and finished the first batch of books on our lists," Poppy said. "Mine made me fall asleep halfway through, but then I woke up and stayed up reading until seven." She nodded proudly.

"You stayed up until seven AM?" I asked in a high-pitched voice. I'd seen this woman take naps in-between her naps.

"No, seven PM." A pause. "Seven PM," she repeated, as if she'd admitted to doing black flips through the cobbled streets.

"Yes, nobody cares," Ava said, her Scottish accent, thicker than usual. She was excited as well. They all were. Usually nothing thrilling happened, except for that last murder and this one.

This had better be the last murder. This was supposed to be a quiet, rural village with a psychotic chicken and lovely scones.

"Ava," Eleanor chided.

"What? Comatose patients go to bed later than Poppy. Now, listen here," she said to me. "I was reading the first book by Carl Scranton, and in it the main character loves hiding places for his precious items. He is very paranoid and doesn't hide anything in his home, but at the cemetery." She wriggled her auburn eyebrows.

"That's the perfect place to bury something," Detective Black said.

"Have you checked the cemetery?" I asked.

Eleanor gasped. "Is that why you were walking around staring at the graves this morning?"

Ava nodded. "Of course. It is my duty as...a member of the book club. Anyway, I didn't find anything suspicious, but still, I wanted to let you know. I'll work on the next book." She didn't await anyone else's turn and rushed off in a cloud of musky perfume.

We all stared at Poppy.

"Seven o'clock isn't too early," she said, pouting.

"Of course not," Eleanor said. "You sleep whenever you want, dear."

And she did. Usually in public places and during moments that required her attention. She had once slept through a play we'd put up right here in the village square during the mayor's birthday. Which would not have been an issue, except she was in it.

It had been the most boring monologue in the history of plays.

"What did you find out?" I asked her.

"I'll tell you what I found out," she started and continued to tell us about the entire plot of the novel, in great detail. It was the first and only novel written by the married couple. It had sold pretty well, but it sounded boring. It could also have been because of the way Poppy told it. Either way, I didn't think there were any clues to be found. Not that I had expected it; this was something the book club women had come up with. I had serious doubts it would lead to anything meaningful, including the titbit that Ava had just given. Still, I'd have to check out the cemetery myself, just to put my mind at ease.

Phoebe had read the second book Carl had written, which also yielded nothing noteworthy, but Eleanor and Lily had read the final book. The book that Rachel had supposedly written. Perhaps that was why I had high hopes that there'd be something meaningful, but there was nothing of interest. It seemed to be a standard mystery novel, but this one contained more action scenes and even a sex scene, which made Lily blush as she mentioned it.

Jessica discussed Sophia's book, in which most characters had issues with their family, or problems with drugs and other things like that. It still said very little about reality. It was impossible to figure out what was important and what not, but I appreciated them relaying what they thought was worth mentioning.

I wrote general truths about people, about love, about pain, and yes, I poured some of myself onto the pages, but nothing that would teach the reader anything about myself. It was difficult to explain to someone else, but that was why I didn't think it would help me find Carl's killer.

"But maybe it will lead you to a clue that in turn will reveal the killer," Detective Black said.

I really hoped so.

Chapter 11

When the women had gone, I was left alone with Christina who was at the counter, tidying up. I still wanted to give her space to figure out her feelings, and so I went upstairs. I wrote for an hour before going next door to walk Bailey. I needed to clear my head, even if it meant going outside, where the sun was. I'd put on a lot of sunscreen. Again. It made me so sticky that someone could probably throw me against the wall, and I'd stay there.

There were a few customers in the shop, and Bailey was lying on the floor. Only his tail moved while I approached him.

I had to look twice when I caught sight of Emblyn dusting one of the shelves with small statues of goddesses. She was so focussed she didn't even notice me.

Nancy was at the counter, ringing up a customer. She was still wearing the golden necklace that Gus had given her. When she was done, she turned to me, and when I nodded towards Emblyn, she said: "Best to keep the enemy close."

I hadn't expected her to take a chance on Emblyn so soon, but it meant that perhaps she'd taken a liking to the girl. Apart from the one stealing incident, she was actually a sweet girl. And lonely. The latter was something we could remedy here in Castlefield.

"I'm glad you are giving her an opportunity to make amends," I said.

"I won't go easy on her, if that's what you're thinking."

"Perish the thought," I said with a grin and grabbed the leash from under the counter. "I'm taking him for a walk, even if it means braving the big fireball in the sky."

"I am so proud of you," she said in an exaggerated tone.

"You should be. This is England, we should be having clouds and rain all 365 days. This is a huge betrayal."

Emblyn looked up as I was leaving, and I winked at her. She beamed back at me.

I was beginning to like her. She'd get along with my aunt just fine.

Bailey trotted alongside me as I walked past the village square. By now Eddie and Sophia were gone, and I suspected he'd taken her for a picnic. It was his go-to date in summer, spring, and even autumn.

I went in the direction of the local park and then I'd walk past a few cottages and make my way back to the church, so I could check out the cemetery. It was unlikely anything was hidden there, but it was on my way.

There were plenty of people in the park, despite the heat. Families with small children were feeding ducks, and there was someone with a fancy camera taking pictures of the two swans in the pond.

I had made it halfway around the pond when, on a bench, was Rachel. She was staring at the water, a frown on her face. But at least she looked better than the day before.

Bailey sniffed around, but I tugged him along towards the murder suspect. What's a mystery author to do?

"Hi," I said. "May I?"

She looked at the bench as if she'd only just noticed it. "Yes, of course," she said and made room for me.

"How are you holding up?" I asked after scratching Bailey's chin. He moved over to Rachel who bent down to stroke his ears.

"You're pretty much the only person who's spoken to me. Well, apart from the police," she said.

"I'm sorry about that. It's because you threatened him. I mean, you did say you were staying here so you could talk to him. Did you ever do that?"

"No. I was still planning on what to say to him, as well as mentally preparing myself. He could be very charming."

"I highly doubt that," Detective Black said.

Me too.

"Can you think of a reason someone would want him dead?"

"Plenty. He was a thief. It wouldn't surprise me if all his manuscripts were stolen. I don't think he had a creative bone in his body," Rachel said. "I also think he enjoyed doing it. Fooling women. He was a user, and he only cared about himself."

I contemplated this.

"Not that I want to speak ill of the dead," she added.

Detective Black scoffed.

A few minutes later I left Rachel to continue brooding while I resumed my walk with Bailey. Normally he was relieved to get some exercise, but it was so hot that he seemed offended that we were even contemplating moving around. He soon changed his tune when we ran into a Beagle.

Eventually we reached the church, and I entered through the iron gate. There were still standing tables and lots of people were taking a moment to chat and have a drink or snack. I had to walk around the church to reach the cemetery. Bailey dutifully followed me as I looked for anything unusual. There were no patches of ground that looked like someone had recently overturned them. It had been a long shot, but still I found myself disappointed.

"The best thing to do when you hit a dead end," Detective Black said, "is to do nothing and let the murder simmer."

"Simmer?"

"Or float? Drift? Ripen? You're the one who does the metaphors. Now, come on, the best way to get your mind off this murder is to get into the fictional one."

"Good point. Come on, Bailey." I turned around and shrieked, not having expected someone to be there.

"Well," Lily said with a scowl, "you're no prize either. I'm sure you pride yourself on being odd, but what are you doing skulking around in the cemetery like some...some...skulker?"

"Impressive vocab," I said dryly.

She narrowed her eyes at me.

"I'm looking for clues. Remember, the one Ava told me about?" I said.

She gasped. "That's right. I already forgot about that. My mind is all over the place, like confetti. You know, I'm having the most terrible day. It started off well enough, with all the excitement brewing over potential clues that we found in the books, but ever since then it's been dreadful."

"That was half an hour ago."

"Exactly. All that dread packed into thirty minutes."

"And what exactly happened that was so awful?" Lily could be a tad dramatic, but only after she drank white wine. Nothing else, just white wine.

"I was planning on returning home, to check out some more about those authors that came here, when I ran into my dear friend Pam, and she talked me into getting an ice cream. It is summer after all, but then I dropped my ice cream and it stained my shirt and Pam laughed. Laughed, I tell you. I can still hear it. Not only that, but the stain probably won't come out of this shirt," she said as she pointed, "which means that this shirt is ruined and from now on will remind me of my failure. Then something even more awful happened when I went on my way home, because I came across Pandora and she was about to chase me, but then she chased a red tabby." She scowled. "A cat was more alluring than me, apparently. Who does that chicken think she is with all those feathers and those eyes?"

"Indeed, ho—"

"And then when I came home, feeling dejected, I bit my tongue, so that was rather disappointing. Also, to make matters worse, I've got a new dining room table. And it's actually not that nice. So there's that. I came back here with my head held high, though, to show everyone how strong I am. And mostly because I'm peckish, and they're handing out sausage rolls."

"You enjoy your white wine?"

She blushed. "How did you know?"

"A hunch." I was about to leave.

"Wait, there was something else I was going to tell you." She took a moment to think. "Ah, yes. The handsome lawyer who bought the Pembroke," she started.

"Yes?"

"There's this woman who keeps going into his house. Sometimes with groceries."

"Kelly I think her name is. She works for him," I said.

"She bought Extra chewing gum on Wednesday morning," she whispered as if it was a major secret.

"How is that important?"

She sighed. "I thought you were supposed to be good at this. Carl popped that chewing gum after every meal, probably because he thought he'd be making out with one of the women here. And yes, I was one of the women he hit on. Not successfully, of course. I'd rather lick a lamp post." She put her hand in front of her mouth. "Did I just say that? I think I've had too much wine."

"You definitely have. But thanks, bye." I picked up Bailey and ran to Nancy's shop so I could drop him off, but I'd barely reached the village square before I started sweating as if I'd run a marathon. I started speed walking instead. I'd soon be in an air-conditioned space, I just had to hang on.

"Wait, can't you just work on your novel instead?" Detective Black said.

I shook my head vigorously.

Emblyn was near the entrance and looked up when I approached her. "Hi, Maggie," she said.

I placed Bailey in her arms and with a frown on my face, continued on to the Pembroke.

"Bye, Maggie," Emblyn called after me.

I LET MYSELF IN WITH the key that Miles had given me. The place was quiet, and I shouted Miles' name. I wasn't sure if Kelly was there, but since Miles was now on holiday, I figured he was doing his own groceries.

I took out my phone to ring Miles, when he came past the staircase.

"Maggie, what a nice—"

"Where's Kelly?" I asked.

"She's off."

"Is she going on holiday, do you know?"

"No, I don't. What's this about?" he asked.

"Call her and get her over here, and I'll call Alistair. We'll need him."

"For what?"

"Do you chew bubble gum?"

"Good heavens, no. That stuff is terrible." He made a face. "What am I? A cow?"

"Then it's very likely that Kelly gave Carl a room in this building. All his belongings will be here. If she didn't get rid of them."

He frowned. "I really hope that is not true."

I called Alistair while Miles called Kelly. Both of them picked up, and both of them were on their way. Kelly had no idea why; Miles had said it was an emergency and nothing more. Technically, it was, so that wasn't a lie.

While we waited for both of them to arrive, I filled him in on what Lily had told me.

"That means his phone could be here as well," he said.

"And that will definitely come in handy. It's quite possible that he texted the killer, or the killer texted him."

"Why would she let him stay here without telling me, though?" Miles asked.

"Apparently he could be charming. I didn't see it, but a lot of women did. It's possible he thought this hotel was available; the website is still running. He probably wanted privacy, to not have anyone see his comings and goings. Maybe because of Wendy, I don't know. But Gregor told us that Carl came here because of a woman. That he told them he was staying with her."

"Maybe she is that woman," Miles said.

"Right."

Kelly was the first to show up. She wasn't how I pictured her to be. She was in her thirties, chubby and pretty. Her hair short, no makeup.

Miles didn't waste any time and questioned her as if she was on the stand. He presented the witness account and fired questions at her. I watched her frown, then burst into tears. He really was something.

Alistair came in just as she was crying on Miles' shoulder.

I filled him in, and we waited for her to calm down.

"Alright, I helped him. He had a room on the second floor," she said.

Miles shook his head.

If someone had secretly let a stranger stay in my home, I'd probably do more than shake my head.

"Why did you help him?" Alistair asked.

She made a face, as if she was tasting something foul. "He—he was my half-brother," she said.

"What?" we all said simultaneously.

"His father had an affair with my mother. He left him and his mother behind to be with us. He had me and my sister and never got in touch with Carl or his mother again. Not that I know of, anyway. Carl contacted me a few years ago, and he was nice at first. But he'd always make these remarks that were designed to make me feel guilty. And it worked. I loaned him a total of five thousand pounds and never got it back. And when he told me he wanted to stay in the Pembroke Hotel, even though I informed him it wasn't a hotel right now, I still felt pressured to give him a room." She glanced at Miles. "I'm so sorry."

Miles touched her shoulder. "Show us the room," he said.

She sighed, probably relieved we would no longer focus on her, and led the way to the second floor. It was the first room on the right. None of the doors were locked, since the hotel wasn't open, and so we could just stroll in.

"Have you touched anything?" Alistair asked.

She shook her head. "No, I've not even been in here. Not even the maids have been in here."

"And why didn't you tell anyone after he died?" I asked.

She teared up again. "Because I felt relieved that he was dead, and then I felt bad about feeling that way. I also didn't want anyone to know that I'd let him stay here. I didn't want to disappoint Miles." She started sobbing again.

Miles pressed his lips together but didn't comfort her this time.

They both lingered near the door while we went inside. There was one suitcase, and packets of bubble gum were scattered across the desk. Other than that, it was surprisingly tidy.

There was no sign of a statuette of a quill, but his phone was charging on his night stand.

Alistair took out gloves and picked up the phone. "Password protected," he said. "I'm sure we'll be able to crack that at the station. Eventually." He sighed.

"He was very vain, you should try his birthday. Do you know it?" I asked Kelly the latter.

She shook her head.

Alistair put it in a clear plastic bag that he apparently always carried around. At least he was prepared. He put the phone in his breast pocket. "I'll take this back to the station. It doesn't appear as if there's anything else, but I'll get a few constables to come pick up his stuff. I'll wait here until they arrive. You guys wait downstairs."

At least we finally had some more clues.

Chapter 12

I waited downstairs with Miles and Kelly. We were in the reception room close to the front door. Kelly was so anxious she started making tea, which left Miles and me alone.

"Are you going to fire her?" I asked.

"Yes," Miles said. "I need to be able to trust someone like her. I can't anymore. It's a shame, though. I liked her."

"She was basically emotionally blackmailed," I said.

"Yes. But it still doesn't change the fact that she should have told me. Especially after he died."

"True." I sighed. "Good help is hard to find. But at least your employee didn't try to murder you," I said, thinking of the events of a few months ago, as I glanced at the now sealed-off death trap behind the wall to my right.

"Luckily you're fine."

"Yes, otherwise who would play your girlfriend, right?"

"Right." He grinned.

Two constables came and got Carl's belongings, including the phone, while Alistair joined us. By now Kelly had returned with a pot of tea, biscuits, and a store-bought cake she had decorated with swirls of chocolate and whipped cream. She was either keeping busy or desperately trying to prove her worth to Miles. Poor girl. But to be fair, if I was in Miles' shoes, I wouldn't be able to trust her either.

"Perhaps we should go to the pub," I said to Alistair, "and discuss everything so far." I needed to organise my thoughts, but most importantly, I needed lunch.

"You'll need to make an official statement at the police station," he said to Kelly.

She turned pale. "I do?"

"Yes," Alistair said.

Miles got up. "Will she be charged with obstruction of justice?"

Kelly gasped as she realised that might happen.

"She has been helpful so far, but I'd like to get her official statement first. We'll go now. Sorry, Maggie. We'll discuss things later," he said.

"I'll go as well," Miles said.

"No, I think it's better if we discuss things without you," Alistair said and eyed Kelly.

She nodded. "I don't think I want to tell it all in front of you again. I'm so sorry I let you down."

Miles put his hands in his pockets. "I understand. And I hope you can understand that I have to let you go."

She nodded again, but started crying.

I glanced at Alistair, whose jaw clenched. He looked like he wanted to be anywhere but here.

Kelly would probably cry the entire way to the police station.

"He might jump out of his own car," Detective Black said.

After a few soothing words from Miles, which didn't help at all, Alistair took her with him. He shot one more glance at me before shutting the front door behind him.

"Well, that was fun," Miles said dryly.

"Do you want to go to the pub? I'll cheer you up with stories about Snowball."

"Who now?"

"My bunny. She can do some tricks," I said.

"Like jump into a preheated oven?"

"Hey!" I punched him on the arm, not hard.

"Okay, I'll remember never to cook you rabbit," he said.

"Very smart. Because otherwise I'll have to train Snowball to attack you."

"I'm so scared." He pretended to shiver.

"Or maybe I should get Pandora to attack you."

Now he really shivered.

WE HAD LUNCH IN THE Rose, where an interested Callum struck up a conversation with Miles, mainly complimenting his sense of style and wanting to know where he worked out.

Miles was handsome, so I figured he got attention like this all the time. He gave Callum enough information to not be rude, then returned his attention to me.

Callum was too gracious to try and hog the conversation after that and left to put our orders in.

"I appreciate that you found out this particular piece of information," Miles started, "but don't you think it's dangerous to put your nose where it doesn't belong?"

I folded my arms. "Murder is everybody's business. We need to know this village is safe. We already have Pandora running around. I mean, if she had hands, many people would have died already." I giggled as I pictured a chicken with arms.

"If someone was willing to get another human out of the way by killing them, then don't you think they could do that again?" Miles asked, still serious.

"Yes, I suppose they could."

"And whereas they won't bump off the police, they might readily dispose of nosey neighbours." He raised an eyebrow. Even when he was telling me what to do, or not to do, he was still fetching. It was unsettling.

"I promise I won't meet anyone at the church late at night, then." I did my best to smile innocently. We were finally getting somewhere with this case. I wasn't going to quit now. I probably couldn't quit.

Oh, boy. Was I really addicted to murder investigations?

"Yes," Detective Black said.

Good to know.

"That's not the point. The killer could be someone you know and trust. Or he might find you alone sometime and take that moment to hurt you. Look, I've seen enough to know that—"

"Yes, yes. I get what you're saying." I leaned forward. "It's just not enough reason for me to stop."

He narrowed his eyes. "Are you just reckless or do you have a death wish?"

"Maybe both," I said defiantly.

He sighed. "You're a handful, aren't you?"

"You're not my keeper, you don't have to worry about me."

"I guess you've just grown on me," he said with a sincere smile.

I smiled back. "Well, I suppose we are friends, so you've earned worry privileges."

"Gee, thanks."

"For our one month friendiversary you'll win a toaster, so there's that."

"Wow, if that's what I win after one month, what do I win after a year?"

"A loin cloth."

He laughed. "You certainly do have a wild imagination."

"You have no idea."

We enjoyed our lunch with some idle chit-chat, which was a nice change from all the murder talk. It also made me miss Christina. We always talked about everything. Perhaps I would say something to her the next time I saw her. I could compliment her dress. Though that might look like I was sucking up to her. I could discuss the murder. No, that topic was too close to Alistair. Maybe I should discuss the migration pattern of the monarch butterfly.

Miles mentioned something about his parents.

"What?"

"Do you want to know anything about my parents before tomorrow?" he asked.

"Yes, actually. Is there anything I should do? Like dress a certain way? Or bring something your parents will appreciate?"

He chuckled. "You don't have to do anything except show up. I just want my parents to see you are real. That should be enough. But if you'd like to put in some effort, then my mum's favourite colour is purple, she loves daffodils, and she doesn't like heavy makeup on women. My dad will probably dislike you no matter what, because you're not a lawyer."

"Lovely," I said.

Miles shot me a dazzling smile. "Have I told you how much I appreciate this?"

I grumbled.

"Do you know what you want in return yet?" he asked in an ominous tone.

"No. And don't worry, I won't make you strip naked and run around the village. It will cause several heart attacks."

"Yours included?"

"I'm sure I'll be fine. Now, let's go, we should get on with the day."

"I'll pay," he said as he got up. "It's the least I could do for what you did today."

"I got your assistant fired," I said as we headed over to Callum so Miles could pay him.

"No, you exposed the truth. That is important. I needed to know I couldn't trust her."

"It's not always that black and white," I said.

"Sometimes it is."

"Come back anytime," Callum said as he handed him the receipt.

"Thank you," Miles said.

"Bye, Call." I waved.

"Have fun," he said with a smirk.

I glared at him. If he was going to spread more gossip, I'd soon get a reputation.

We stepped outside into the blazing heat again, and I had to fight the urge to run back inside. I really hated this heat.

"Will you spend time at the library today?" Miles asked.

"No, I'll do some writing. I might stop by tomorrow afternoon, though."

"Okay, see you then." He gave me an unexpected kiss on the cheek and walked off. He passed Alistair. They both stopped and chatted briefly before Alistair made his way over to me.

By then I was already sick of the heat. "Do you mind finding some shade while we talk?" I asked him.

"Not at all," he said. "Did you have a nice lunch with Miles?"

"I did. You know, I still need to think of something I want in return for pretending to be his girlfriend. Can you think of anything good?"

"The promise that he'll never ask you to do something like that again?"

I laughed. "I'm sure he won't ever ask me to do something like that after tomorrow. Now that he's back, are you guys spending a lot of time together?"

"We have spent some time together, but he's very busy with his work. This is his first week off, and now there's a murder that is keeping me occupied. But it's a small village and that helps. I'm glad he moved back. Now I've got two good friends," he said and as one corner of his mouth turned up.

Near the park was a bench that was hidden by the shadow of the oak tree behind it. We took refuge there. It was quiet since most people were at the village square, which we could partially see from here.

"If we are all friends, then it shouldn't matter that I'm having dinner with his parents tomorrow, right?"

Alistair narrowed his eyes at me, then sighed. "What do you want me to say?"

"Nothing. Never mind. Tell me if you found out anything new about the case. Did you get into his phone?"

"I did. You were right. His code was his birthday. Very stupid, but it worked in our favour. First of all, there were a lot of messages from Wendy. She was clearly not over him at all. She was madly in love and didn't like it when he broke up with her. She said some creepy things about how nobody else could have him."

"Yikes."

"And that leads me to Gregor. Carl sent him a text message, asking for him to bring his briefcase—empty, of course—but wouldn't say why. It was the last message he sent. Which means, that Gregor was the last to see him alive."

"Only if he's the killer."

"Either way," Alistair said. "We're going to talk to them both. It's suspicious, but so far it doesn't prove anything."

"Hopefully we'll be able to get somewhere when we ask them."

"Yes, but we should talk to them separately."

"Agreed." I felt like I truly was his colleague, and it felt nice.

"Yes," Detective Black said, "who knew that a mystery author would enjoy solving a mystery?"

Chapter 13

As we headed in the direction of the B&B, we spotted Wendy crossing the street. We stopped and watched her buy a muffin. When she sat down on a bench in the shade, we made our way over. The muscles in her neck and shoulders tensed as soon as we made eye contact.

I sat down next to her while Alistair remained standing.

"What is it now?" she asked.

Alistair took a picture out of his breast pocket. It was a printed screenshot of the text message she'd sent Carl.

She turned red. "So what? I had a desperate moment. It happens to the best of us."

I almost snorted.

"It gives you a motive," Alistair said. "And I don't like being lied to when conducting a murder investigation."

She sighed and looked deflated. Some of her hostility had apparently been let out along with her breath. "I'm sorry. It was just embarrassing to admit, especially in front of Gregor. It was supposed to be a fling, which is what I kept telling myself, but I found that Carl's sweet lies were getting to me. I liked hearing I was beautiful, sexy, and somewhere along the line I started craving the feeling that Carl gave me. The feeling that I mattered. I know it was all pretend for him, which is why it was so stupid. He turned me into a pathetic excuse of a woman." She sighed. "It would be easy to blame Gregor, but we've both been bad communicators."

"Did Carl ever respond to your text messages?" I asked.

She shook her head. "Not if you include him very obviously flirting with other women in front of me. I was a nuisance to him, I'm sure. And I can't blame him. Men like him want the chase, they don't like it when women make it too easy."

I said nothing, certain she was right. About Carl, anyway.

"Did you go and see him that night?" Alistair asked.

Wendy looked up and shook her head. "I took my sleeping tablets. It took me a while to find them. My insomnia had gotten worse ever since Carl broke up with me. Gregor saw me take them."

"She could have spat them out later," Detective Black said. "It doesn't rule her out completely."

Or Gregor, I thought.

"And did Gregor go to bed at the same time as you?" Alistair asked, knowing the answer already.

"No, but I can't be certain how long he stayed up. Look, DS Ashworth. I really think you're barking up the wrong tree. Gregor would never do such a thing, nor I."

"Unfortunately, we can't take your word for it. People who are capable of murder are also very capable of lying." He flipped his notebook shut. "Thanks for your time, Miss Cohen."

We left her with her muffin that was dangerously close to falling out of her hand. She didn't even seem to notice, as she stared off in the distance.

"If she took those sleeping tablets, it means that Gregor doesn't have an alibi. Then again, she could have pretended to take the tablets and that means she doesn't have an alibi either," I said. "Technically, they could have been in it together."

"I know, but let's see what Gregor has to say about the briefcase. It's not like Gregor texted Carl, and I can't imagine what Carl needed an empty briefcase for so late at night." We headed to the B&B where Mrs Suzuki informed us that Gregor had gone off to the pub.

I could hardly blame him for wanting some alcohol considering the fact that his whole life had just been turned upside down.

Although, he'd get no sympathy from me if he turned out to be the killer.

It was early and hot, so the pub wasn't busy. Gregor was in a dark corner, nursing a beer. He looked like he was carrying the entire world on his shoulders. Alistair and I exchanged a look before approaching him.

"Mind if we sit?" I asked with a smile, hoping to bring some brightness in his gloomy corner.

He grunted, which we took as an affirmative.

"How are you holding up?" I asked, thinking a little interest would do no harm.

Gregor scoffed. "My only friend in the world got murdered, my wife cheated on me with him, and I keep thinking that this would make a great story. What is wrong with me?" He rubbed his face.

"That's just your writer's mind. They are always very weird. Don't worry about it."

He looked up at me and managed a small smile.

Alistair cleared his throat. "During our first chat you said you had seen Carl last at the pub. But we know that he messaged you, asking for your briefcase."

"So you found his phone? Well, I—yes, he did ask me for that. My briefcase, but emptied out. He said he needed it for something, but wouldn't say what."

"And you brought it to him?"

"No, he came to the B&B."

"So you saw him then?"

Gregor looked down. "Sorry I didn't tell you, but yeah. It was just so weird, and he swore me to secrecy."

"Why do you think he did that?"

"I figured he had knocked someone up and had to bribe her or something." Gregor blushed.

"Had that happened before?" I asked.

"Yes. Two years ago. He bribed the woman to—err—take care of it."

"Honourable guy," I said.

"I know. He told me after it had happened, so there was nothing to be done. But the woman wouldn't have done it if she didn't want to get rid of it too."

"Why were you friends with him?" I asked. I just couldn't comprehend it at all.

"He was a really good guy. He was funny, supportive, smart. I know you've seen the worst of him, but he's actually charming."

"Serial killers are charming," I said. "It sounds to me like he was good at manipulating people."

Gregor sighed. "I'm starting to think that too."

"So, you were the last to see him," Alistair said, drumming his fingers on the table.

"No, the killer saw him last. Not me. I handed him the briefcase, tried to get more information, but he turned around and left."

"And then what did you do?"

"I went up to bed."

"And your wife was there?" Alistair asked.

"Of course she was there. She had taken sleeping tablets. I saw her take them." Gregor shifted in his seat. "Am I under arrest?"

"Not yet." Alistair got up, and I followed suit. "I'll be in touch." Then he turned and left, with me on his heels.

"Come on, this way," he said to me, and we went to the park to find a bench that overlooked the pond. It was partially covered by the shade of an oak tree. Alistair let me sit in the shade, even though he was wearing a suit. My objections didn't change his mind.

"Suck-up," Detective Black said.

Clearly my detective had something to learn.

"So, Sherlock, what do you think?" Alistair asked and put his arm on the back of the bench as he turned to me.

"I think Gregor is the most likely suspect of them both. Even if Wendy didn't take sleeping tablets, she would have had to leave the bed after Gregor returned. Although, technically, if he was a heavy sleeper, she could have pulled it off."

"But Gregor seemed genuinely surprised about the affair, and what else could his motive be?" Alistair asked. "Besides, we can speculate all we want; we need proof."

"Do you know anything else about Carl? Did he have a will?"

"His lawyer is on holiday, we left a message for him. He should get back to us soon. If he did have one, I'm curious who he left everything to. He didn't seem to have anyone who cared for him."

"Except Gregor."

"Yeah, but he had an affair with his wife. He clearly only cared about himself."

"True. So what's next?" I asked.

Pandora shot off towards a couple of ducks, chasing them away from the edge of the pond. She stopped, turned her head and looked right at us.

"Oh, boy. I hope she doesn't want a rematch with you," I said.

"I can handle her." He stared at her.

She stared back.

Tumbleweed rolled by. Oh, wait, that was just in my imagination.

She started drawing back her one foot like a bull, ready to attack.

Alistair grunted. "It's too hot to fight a chicken." He glanced at me. "Wow, never thought I'd say that."

She advanced.

I pulled my legs up on the bench, though I was sure she could jump up if she fluttered her wings hard enough.

Alistair got up and casually strolled her way. He clearly had a death wish, the daredevil.

They met halfway when Pandora abruptly came to a halt and nearly tripped over herself. They just stared at each other and then, as if hit by a bolt of thunder, she dashed off.

I started clapping. How did he do that? Only Nancy had that kind of power. Well, until now. I had to start practising my death stare in the mirror soon. I couldn't be left behind.

"Very impressive," I said as he returned.

"You pick up a thing or two when dealing with murderers."

"I bet."

He sat back down next to me.

"You know, I could use your intimidation skills."

"You could?"

"Meet me outside the Wicked Bookworm at six this evening."

"Should I be wearing a ski mask?" He grinned.

"It's nothing nefarious, I assure you."

"We could have dinner afterwards? At my place?" His eyes searched my face.

I swallowed.

"Just say yes," Detective Black said. "Don't even pretend you don't want this. You're practically drooling."

"Okay," I said. "As friends."

"Of course. Friends. I'll even give you a high five after dessert, if you want."

I smiled. "Okay. I'll see you tonight. I gotta go back now. Detective Black is getting jealous."

"Oh, we don't want that, do we?"

"No, he'll not listen to a word I write otherwise." I chuckled.

"Damn straight," Detective Black said.

When I returned to the Wicked Bookworm, Christina was just ringing up a customer. It was otherwise quiet in the shop, and when the customer left, I decided to see if she was ready to strike up a conversation. As I approached, my palms got sweaty, and it had nothing to do with the weather.

"Hey," I said to her. Mainly because I couldn't think of anything else.

"Hey," she said. "How's the murder investigation going?"

Nice, we were talking.

"I sort of feel like I'm following clues around, always chasing facts or hunches. But I suppose that makes it interesting," I said. "That's what Detective Black goes through as well."

"But with less heart-shaped eyes directed at a certain detective," he said.

"And you're investigating with Alistair?" she asked. There was no tone, but it was still a dangerous question.

"Yes, though we're not—I mean, I'm basically just asking people some questions, that's all."

She nodded slowly as she observed my face. "It seems to make you happy. Spending time with him."

Before I could react, she headed over to a new customer, whom I hadn't even seen entering.

Was that a good thing? Or a bad thing? Was she just stating something?

I rubbed my temple and headed upstairs so I could write.

"Finally," Detective Black said. "I'm in the mood for fictional murder and mayhem."

Chapter 14

I went down around six, which was just when Christina and Eddie closed the shop. I slipped out through the back and walked around to meet up with Alistair. He was on the pavement between my shop and Nancy's. He was dressed the same, though he had put on some extra cologne, which I noticed as I approached. I couldn't blame him; with this weather I had used my deodorant three times already.

His lips curled into a smile as he spotted me.

"Thanks for coming," I said.

"No problem. Where are we going?"

"I want to visit Gus and see if I can get him to open up about my aunt."

"Oh, boy," Detective Black said. "No good can come of that."

"Are you sure that's wise?" Alistair asked.

"Nancy is still very upset about it, I can tell. I think he broke her heart, and he didn't give her a reason why. Maybe we can still get that explanation for her, so we can give her some closure. If not, I'll have at least tried."

"What makes you think he'll tell you the truth? He might not know the reason himself, not fully. Or perhaps it's something embarrassing or painful."

"I'm not expecting anything, but I want to try. She would do the same for me."

Alistair scoffed. "She'd probably attack anyone who'd break your heart, with a broom."

"More like with a chainsaw, but yeah. Did you know that chainsaws were actually invented to assist with childbirth back in the day? When a lot of women died in childbirth, the male doctors—they had to be men in order to come up with this—thought it might be handy to saw the pelvic bone and make it 'easier' for the baby to come out. They did this during child birth, by the way. Without anaesthesia."

Alistair winced.

"But it would take quite some time, so they basically came up with a mini chainsaw that would work faster."

"How do you know this?"

"Research," I said. "Just like how I know what a corpse flower is. And that they smell terrible."

Alistair grinned. "Aren't you supposed to research murder stuff? Like poisons? Causes of death?"

"I also know plenty about that. If anyone saw my browser history, they'd think I was a serial killer. And in a way, I am. I just couldn't kill an actual person. I still don't understand how some people do that. I still feel guilty about watching a neighbourhood kid step on snails while all I did was yell at him. I was a child myself, but it still bothers me."

"Who did that then?"

"I don't remember. I don't think it was anyone I went to class with. It was a long time ago."

"Well, you shouldn't feel guilty, but it's a good thing that you care that much. It means you're a good person. I've learned that there are very disturbing people out there, and that usually those people seem, and sometimes are, otherwise normal.

Some people are born killers, some experience things that make them into killers, and some people are pushed into a corner and believe that murder is the solution."

"Yes, I know. I've read up on a lot of information about serial killers, and even 'normal' killers, but I still don't truly understand that lack of emotion. But like you say, that's probably a good thing." I couldn't help but think about what Christina had told me about Alistair and his partner back in London. That was undoubtedly something his psychologist was helping him with as well.

"The same with people who kill in self-defence," I add. "It would be odd if that person didn't really care at all."

Alistair cast a glance in my direction. "Right."

"In fact, it would be normal if they did." I stopped as we reached The Antique Shoppe. "Oh, look. We're here." Without awaiting any reply that might or might not have come, I knocked on the door to Gus' shop. He would probably be in the back, finishing up for the evening. The 'closed' sign was already turned.

He came out from behind the curtain to the back of his shop and froze for a moment as he stared at me. Then he glanced at Alistair and rushed over.

"See, it's good to bring a detective along," Detective Black said. "Otherwise he'd have turned around and hid."

He was probably right.

Gus took a moment to take the keys from his trouser pocket and unlocked the door slowly.

I eyed Alistair as impatience bubbled to the surface and took the shape of a frown. He, however, seemed unperturbed.

"Detective, Maggie, what can I do for you?" he asked with a forced cheerfulness.

"May we come in, please?" I asked.

He stepped aside to let us through. "Is this about the murder? All those mystery authors visited my shop at some point, according to my assistant, but I haven't spoken to them or seen anything suspicious."

We remained standing in the middle of the crowded shop. It was filled with antique bits and pieces. Baskets, mirrors, combs, dolls, tea cups, a typewriter—oh my, a typewriter!

"Down girl," Detective Black said.

Right, focus.

"Actually, this is about my aunt." I smiled because I wanted to give him a false sense of security; if he turned out to be a jerk, I would have to pull a Poppy and sit on him.

"Right," he said and looked at the floor. "Look, I do really like her. A lot, actually. Things just didn't work out."

"It's just that I think she would benefit from some closure." I wanted to tell him how upset she was, but I couldn't. I knew she wouldn't want him to know about that, and if the roles were reversed, I wouldn't want the guy who jilted me knowing how upset I was.

Gus scratched his head and started pacing around. I glanced at Alistair.

"You don't have to tell us the reason," Alistair said, "but perhaps you can tell Nancy."

At this he looked pained. He shook his head sadly and sighed. From his trouser pocket he retrieved an amethyst stone. "She gave me this to help me sleep. I have it on me all the time; it reminds me of her. She was so sweet and caring."

Alistair made what sounded like a snort, then covered it with a cough.

I glared at him.

"Look, you clearly have feelings for her. If that's the case, then why end things so abruptly?"

"What were you afraid of?" Alistair asked. "Of letting her down? Worried she could do better?"

I studied Alistair's face, but he kept his eyes on Gus. Was that what he was worried about with me? Or was he just speaking from a past experience?

"Maybe both," Detective Black said.

Gus took off his small round glasses and stared at them. "The doctor gave me six months."

I let out a gasp. I hadn't seen that coming.

We were both too shocked to say anything.

"I am sure you're thinking that it's a good reason to keep seeing her, make the most of it. But that would be selfish, because what about the aftermath? What about those final moments? It's not like we've been together for years. This way, things would stay light and casual. And so would the impact."

"You clearly don't know my aunt, if that's what you think. She is fierce when it comes to love, and I believe she loves you. I'm really sorry you're going through this, but please don't underestimate Nancy. Give her a chance. She'll never forgive you if you don't at least do that."

He looked up at me. "I'll think about it. That's the best I can do."

"Thank you. And I really am sorry," I said.

He nodded.

We left quietly and took a moment to process everything before strolling back in the direction of Alistair's. It was still light out and it was quiet on the street. Most people were having dinner right about now.

"That was quite something," Alistair said.

"Do you think he'll tell her the truth?"

"Yes."

"How do you know?" I asked.

"Because he's in love with her. Despite everything, a chance to be with her is still too enticing."

We looked at each other.

"Do you think they'll get together?"

"I hope so."

I looked ahead. "I think so. If it's meant to be, then they will find a way."

I HELPED ALISTAIR COOK a vegetarian lasagna, and while it was in the oven, we made an apple pie. It looked so delicious I wanted to forget all about the lasagna and just skip to dessert. It was so delightfully normal to do something like this with him.

The lasagna still had ten minutes to go, so we sat in the garden with home-made lemonade.

"Are your parents happy that you're back?"

"My mum is excited. I go out to the farm every now and then. Even though she's retired, she's keeping herself entertained. My dad is still very busy with the farm, so he's the same as always. I think he's a bit disappointed I didn't stay in London."

"Did he say that?" I asked.

"No, but I can tell. He'll get over it, I'm sure."

"Of course. I'm sure he will realise that it's not about what sounds cool, but what makes you happy. He didn't become a farmer because of what other people thought of him. He did it because it's his passion."

"Actually, he did it because his dad expected it of him."

"Really?" I asked.

"No, I'm just kidding. He does really love farming."

"Well, there you go."

He smiled. "You make things sound so simple."

"Things are simple. People make them complicated."

"I suppose so. I definitely should have come home as soon as I realised that I wasn't happy in London. Everything there was fast and hard. I did my best to keep up, but in the end I just became someone I wasn't. It was surprisingly easy to lie to myself, just because I was afraid of change. Afraid of admitting I'd made a mistake." He shook his head. "I was so stupid."

"You weren't stupid. You were scared."

He made a face. "That's even worse."

"How so? Oh, let me guess...you're a man, you're not supposed to be scared. You're supposed to wrestle boars with your bare hands and then bring them home to eat. And when someone hurts you, you're not supposed to cry, right? Otherwise your tears will melt your face."

He laughed. "Something like that."

"And that is why people make things complicated. We come up with all these 'rules' and thoughts of how things should be, what they should look like, and then we desperately struggle to fit that image. It just sets us up to be miserable. People don't fit into boxes. We are what we are. And we are lots of different things all in one."

He stared at me. "You're quite wise."

"It's the writer in me."

"Speaking of which, when is the next book coming out?"

"You read the last one already?"

"Of course."

My pulse quickened as it always did when I asked people this question. "Did you like it?"

"No."

My eyes widened. "No?"

"No, I loved it."

I let out the breath I was holding and playfully punched his arm. "Don't do that again, you nearly gave me a heart attack."

"Does my opinion matter that much?"

"Yes," I said without thinking.

He gave a slow, sexy smile.

"Shut up," I said and took a sip of my lemonade.

The oven dinged and Alistair got up to get us our food. We would be eating outside. At least he knew me well enough to not bring out a salad. That was food fit for a bunny, not a Maggie.

A moment later we were eating and discussing the Summer Festival so far. Apparently Nancy had joined the flower arranging while Emblyn was minding the shop—a huge step forward for Nancy—and she had sprayed the twigs and flowers black and basically made a goth version. Then she had wailed about how love was a curse and everybody should quit while they were ahead. Alistair had heard this from Dawn, the postwoman and Ava's wife.

Oh, poor Nancy. I hoped Gus would tell her the truth soon. "You're taking part in gossip already. Very good."

"It's not very difficult. Dawn tells everybody everything. I think it's a compulsion."

"That wouldn't surprise me. But it would probably be that way for almost everyone here. They'd have to start a Gossip Anonymous support group."

"And that would then turn out to be a group where everyone gossips."

My lips curled into a smile. "Definitely."

After dinner, I helped Alistair clean the kitchen, which also made me feel like we were a married couple. It didn't feel weird, though. It felt like it had always been like this. And thinking back to when we were teens and spent that one day together, it had felt like that as well. Weird.

"Alright, come with me," Alistair said when we were done, "I want to show you my office now."

I followed him to the front of the house where we entered the door to the right of the staircase. It was a room with three large bookcases and two armchairs placed near them with a small table in between. Perfect for reading. There was a fireplace that wasn't burning. A desk by the window, a tray with alcohol, and a record player in the corner.

"I love it," I said.

"Please," Detective Black said, "Someone shows you a large bookcase, and you're hooked."

"Look," Alistair said and pointed at a row with my Detective Black novels.

"Okay, I like him a bit more now," Detective Black said.

"That's awesome. Do you want me to sign them?"

"Oh, yes." He broke out in a wide smile and hurried to his desk to get a pen.

I grabbed half of the books and sat down while Alistair grabbed the other half and put them on the table between our armchairs. The books looked like he'd read them multiple times. Was that because he liked the books that much or because I had written them? Perhaps I was thinking too much of it.

I signed each and every one with a different general message or a quote. I knew a lot since I had done a few signings. Alistair got up to turn on the record player while I finished signing the last two books. Now that he wasn't looking, I wrote a more personal message:

"The funny thing about the heart is a soft heart is a strong heart, and a hard heart is a weak heart."

I got that quote from a book called *Healology,* and it seemed to fit our earlier discussion.

Alistair returned now that he'd put on a slow song by Dolly Parton. I had not seen that coming, but I liked it. She had some good songs.

He stopped in front of me and held out his hand.

I wasn't sure if it was a good idea, but I gave him my hand anyway. He pulled me up and moved to the middle of the room. With surprising grace he pulled me into his arms, and we started swaying.

When I got too nervous from staring into his eyes, I brushed my cheek against his and closed my eyes. It was nice to be held by him. It felt like home.

Chapter 15

It was dark when Alistair walked me home. I assured him he didn't need to, but he hadn't taken no for an answer. We had avoided the topic of murder up until now, but I was itching to review the case so far.

"So, what are the clues we have?" I asked, but didn't allow Alistair to answer. "We have a very flirty and manuscript-stealing Carl. We have a lover who desperately wants him back, a best friend who seemingly didn't know about the affair and brought him an empty briefcase right before his murder, and a missing prize that was the murder weapon. Oh, and his half-sister was pretty much blackmailed into letting him stay in the Pembroke."

"That pretty much sums it up, yes," Alistair said.

"But we don't have any evidence, and the motives aren't strong enough. Not yet, anyway." At that moment a pleasant breeze cooled the air significantly. I stopped and spread my arms as I enjoyed the feeling with my eyes closed.

"What are you doing?"

"Feeling the wind on my face always makes me feel alive."

"And so you just stand here in the middle of the street?"

"Sometimes," I said.

"What if someone sees you?"

"What does that matter? Really, the only thoughts I care about are from the people I respect and know respect me. Besides, you have to live a little. This feels nice. You should try it."

"I'm good," he said.

I lowered my arms and turned to him. "You should be more like Pandora and do what you want."

"We can't always do whatever we feel like. Or get what we want." He gave me a look.

I stared at him, at a loss for words.

"Do you want me to throw a dictionary at you?" Detective Black asked.

"Some things take time," I said. "And it will be worth it."

He nodded. "Of that I'm sure."

When we reached the door to my flat, Alistair gave me a swift kiss on the cheek. I went up with a grin that was hard to wipe off my face.

The flat was dark and Christina was clearly already sleeping. It was late, and I'd completely lost track of time at Alistair's. I took a shower and then went to bed. I fell asleep within ten minutes.

THAT FRIDAY MORNING Christina and I had breakfast together again. We discussed some general stuff about the Summer Festival. Today would be the water games. The village square had buckets filled with water balloons and water guns and people had free rein to grab them and target anyone they wished. Which meant that it was also the day that most elderly avoided the market and the village square.

It was not because they were afraid of getting wet or injured. It was simply that they got too competitive. Poppy had gone full Rambo last year and together with a few of the other older women, she had come up with an assault plan that had taken out dozens of kids and unsuspecting market browsers. In her enthusiasm she had even attacked Harold, a pregnant lady, and a puppy. When she had attempted to dive and roll, she broke her ankle.

She had been banned from the water games ever since.

I shared that particular information with Christina who managed to give me a smile. She had the day off from working at the Wicked Bookworm and was going to spend it outside.

I, on the other hand, was going to spend it indoors, working on my latest novel.

"Yay," Detective Black said in a serious tone, which made him sound sarcastic.

"I'll see you later then." Christina left after we had cleared the table.

"Bye." We would be okay, I knew. Though I was afraid to cheer too soon.

Just as I sat down at my desk, my phone buzzed. It was a text message from Alistair. He had news and was on his way. I didn't hesitate and grabbed a red handbag, since my dress didn't have pockets, and rushed downstairs. Just as I opened the door to the bookshop, Alistair emerged from behind a bookcase and stopped when he spotted me.

He glanced around, knowing that people were always eavesdropping in public places. And even public places that were supposed to be private. Once, a phone call in the pub's bathroom led to the rumour about someone having an STD. Never mind that the call had really been about SATs.

I held open the door and nodded for him to come over. I shut the door behind him. We could go upstairs to my flat, but I had the feeling we were about to head out soon.

"What happened?" I asked.

"Carl Scranton's solicitor rang me in the middle of the night, due to the time difference, and told me that Gregor is the sole beneficiary of Carl's will."

My eyes widened. "Really? The friend whose wife he cheated with? Wow."

"Yes, well, it gives Gregor a pretty big motive. Two, actually, since we know from the phone messages that his wife still wanted Carl. If Gregor found out..." his voice trailed off. "And we know that he got a message from Carl to meet him with the briefcase. We have actual evidence that he was the last to see him. Assuming he is the killer, of course."

"So you're going to arrest him?"

"Yes. I know you can't come along to the station, but I figure you wanted to be there when I do it. I'm heading over now. I want to ask him some questions first."

"Of course. Let's go."

Alistair smiled. "I'm glad to see you so excited."

"This could mean he confesses and then we'll have solved a case together. That's pretty cool, Watson."

"It is, Sherlock. The game is afoot."

WENDY AND GREGOR WERE having breakfast in the B&B. Mrs Suzuki let us in with wide eyes and followed us with interest. It was clear that she knew something was up. Perhaps she could feel the tension emanating from us both. Or maybe it was just me. I'd never been this close to an arrest. Apart from the previous murder, but I had been fighting for my life, so I didn't really get to enjoy that. Then there were the times that Nancy had been taken in, mainly for assault. Once for public urination.

They both froze when their gazes landed on us. They were the only ones having breakfast right now. I wondered if Sophie was having breakfast with Eddie or if she was still asleep.

"This is harassment," Wendy started.

I was surprised to see them having breakfast together.

"It could be they're dependent on each other. Some people want to suffer together, because they believe it's the best they can do," Detective Black said.

Was that why they had been close to Carl? He wasn't exactly a good friend. Even if Gregor seemed to think—or act—like he was.

"Did either of you know anything about Carl Scranton's will?" Alistair asked.

Wendy put down her spoon and shoved away her bowl of yogurt.

Gregor was still holding his fork and had a few sausages left on his plate. He had a defeated look about him. As if he was just going to go with the flow and didn't have the energy to worry about stuff. Wendy, however, had an aggressive look in her eyes. She also looked like she hadn't slept well in a while; she had dark circles around her eyes and her skin was paler than usual.

"No, of course not," Gregor said. "I mean, I don't even think he had one."

"You think we killed him for his money?" she said. "We wouldn't do that. We cared about him."

Gregor eyed his wife. "Some of us more than appropriate," he muttered.

She had the decency to look down at the table.

"So you would be surprised if I told you that one of you is the sole beneficiary of his will," Alistair said.

Their heads shot up, their eyes wide. They stared at Alistair then at each other.

"Wh—who is the beneficiary?" Wendy asked softly, as if she was afraid the words would break as soon as they left her lips.

"Gregor is," Alistair said.

Gregor dropped his fork. It clattered against his plate. He leaned back with his mouth open. "Are you serious?"

Alistair nodded.

"Considering the fact that he also texted you last, and your wife wanted him back, I'm arresting you for the suspicion of murdering Carl Scranton, and we will have a formal interview at the station."

Wendy gasped. "No, please."

Alistair motioned for Gregor to get up, and he did. Alistair read him his rights and even handcuffed him. That would definitely not go unnoticed. They went outside where Alistair had parked his Beetle.

Wendy and I followed them. I stayed behind, hoping I could chat with Wendy and find out some more information. I wanted to do something useful while Alistair was taking Gregor in. It was very possible that he was the killer, but it was equally possible that he was not. It all seemed a bit convenient. Also, what about the briefcase?

Wendy started sobbing while she scrunched up her face, but there were no tears. It was like she had all these emotions and no idea where to put them.

Mrs Suzuki hurried back into the B&B, quite possibly to phone in this new piece of gossip.

"Come on," I said to Wendy. "Why don't we sit in the garden with something to drink and chat?"

She looked at me as if she'd only just realised I was there. Her mouth became a harsh line and her eyes narrowed.

"If she tries to punch you, kick her in the shin," Detective Black said.

I braced myself; she looked ready to strike.

Her shoulders slumped. "Fine," she said. Her anger had left her body like air from a balloon.

Mrs Suzuki was not on the phone when we entered the kitchen, but instead had two mugs of steaming tea at the ready. "There, you go and relax in the garden." She handed us the mugs.

There were some clouds that occasionally hid the sun, and it was two degrees cooler than the day before, but it was still warm, and it would only get hotter. Tea, it seemed, was always the go-to drink in a time of crisis, even in the blazing heat.

Technically, tea cooled the body temperature, but still, I wasn't sure if I could swallow this.

We sat on the bench that we'd found Gregor and Wendy on the first time we visited. This time there was nobody else in the garden; it was still early.

The fact that Wendy had seemed convinced that Gregor hadn't done it made me wonder if she knew who had. Also, their relationship was odd. She had an affair, pretended not to care, yet at the same time, she clearly still loved Gregor. So what exactly was the deal?

"You were having breakfast together," I said and hoped that was enough to get her to start talking.

"A few comments here and there should do the trick. She has nobody else to talk to. She's probably desperate." Detective Black was beside me.

She nodded and blew on her tea. "It was probably a good thing that Gregor found out. Usually we don't talk about our feelings. We just go on and on, taking each other for granted. Taking everything for granted. Carl made me feel special and beautiful. He was good at saying exactly what you wanted to hear." She took a sip of her tea.

"After Gregor found out, we had a huge fight. It wasn't pleasant, but I think it was good. We got everything out in the open. Not even just recent things, but also things from way back. We laid it all out on the table. Afterwards, we were both relieved. Things were different, but not necessarily worse. We've been communicating ever since. Of course, he hasn't forgiven me, yet. But we're working on it."

She scrunched up her face again. "And now he's gone."

"Do you think he killed Carl?"

"No, no, not at all." She grabbed my wrist. "He's not the kind of guy to do something like that. Even if he had known, which he didn't, then he would never have done something so awful."

"What would he have done, do you think?"

"I don't know. I think he would have gone over to talk about it with Carl, but then lost the nerve and ended up pretending everything was fine." She smiled wryly. "That would be typically Gregor. Or at least, the Gregor before we started talking about things."

"Someone killed Carl," I said.

Her eyes widened. "I realise that, Margie, but it's not Gregor. I really think it's Sophia. She was always following him around like a puppy."

"It's Maggie," I said.

"Who is?"

"I am." I did my best to give her a stern look.

"Right, Maggie," she said in a slightly annoyed tone. "Just go sniff around Sophia, and I'm sure you'll find something. You're helping the police, aren't you?"

She was close to adding 'make yourself useful,' no doubt.

"Fine, I'll look into it. But if her following him around like a puppy is the only thing you've got—" I said, my voice trailing off.

"Well, I can't do your work for you. Although, maybe I should." She raised her eyebrows.

"That is too dangerous," I said.

"You're doing it." She looked at me as if I couldn't even tie my shoelaces on my own.

I folded my arms. "I'm a trained professional." *Sort of.*

Detective Black snorted. "In what? Getting papercuts?"

"Look, do you have any other suspects? Or reasons why you think it's Sophia?" Which I really hoped it wasn't. Eddie would be heartbroken.

"I did once hear her over the phone. Sophia, I mean." Wendy tapped her chin as she recalled the event. "She was talking about not pursuing a lawsuit of some kind. She didn't want to go after someone. Instead she had convinced him to work with her. She wouldn't say who 'he' was, though."

"Do you think it was Carl?"

She shrugged. "Either she was running from someone or running towards someone."

"What's that supposed to mean?"

She sighed impatiently. "She always gave me the impression that she was either hanging around because of some sort of mission, or that she was there to hide from someone. Like, she was never truly herself. I can't explain it. Perhaps it makes no sense."

"Wendy may be a complicated woman, but I don't think she's a nonsensical one," Detective Black said.

Sophia had dyed her hair. Perhaps it was so she wouldn't be recognised. My eyes widened as I recalled the bruises. What if she had an abusive husband she was running from? What if Carl had been taking advantage of that and played the protective hero? What if that had gotten him killed? Or what if Sophia had realised he was using her and snapped?

Still too many possibilities, but it was an angle worth pursuing.

"Thanks, Wendy. I promise I'll look into it." She still had her hand on my wrist, so I gave it a squeeze and then put her hand on her own knee. With a polite nod, I got up and walked around the side of the B&B, leaving through the gate.

For a second I thought she'd call after me, but she didn't. She had to be lonely, but I hoped it wouldn't mean she'd go snooping on her own. She was not the type to ask veiled questions.

I looked down at the tea mug I was still holding. It was not my proudest moment, but I simply put it down outside the gate and hurried off. I had some serious digging to do.

Chapter 16

Sophia hadn't been at the B&B, and Eddie was working. I had no idea what she would be up to in her spare time. I didn't want to ask Eddie for her number because he'd ask why, not to mention that I wanted to catch her off guard. If she knew she was meeting up with me, she would be more guarded than if I happened to run into her.

The only place I could think of was the park. There was plenty of shade, and it would be much nicer to hang out there than in the B&B. It was either the park or the pub. I went to the park first.

It wasn't too busy, but several people had laid down picnic blankets or beach towels on the grass. Some were sunbathing—something I couldn't do; I'd reflect the sunlight—and some people were covered by the oak trees' shade. It took me a while to spot Sophia, but there she was: in a sundress, while on her laptop.

"Something you should be doing," Detective Black said.

"Bite me," I muttered as I approached her.

She looked up and smiled when she saw it was me. "Hi, Maggie. Nice temperature, isn't it? There's a breeze today." Her sunglasses covered her eyes. I didn't like that. I wanted to be able to see people's eyes when I talked to them. I always felt like a vital part of communication was missing when people had shades on.

"May I?" I indicated the picnic blanket.

"Of course. Is everything okay? Did you find anything out about the murder?" She moved her bottle of water and wrapped sandwich, so I could sit next to her. She also shut her laptop and gave me her full attention.

I bit my lip, unsure how to start. "The police arrested Gregor."

"Gregor? Oh, no. Did he really do it? I can't imagine so."

"He's inheriting everything from Carl, and he met up with him right before his murder. He gave him a briefcase."

"With what?"

"Nothing. It was an empty briefcase."

She turned to me and took off her sunglasses. "How intriguing." Then she clasped her hand in front of her mouth. "I'm sorry. How terribly macabre of me."

"We are mystery authors, after all. I won't hold that against you."

"Thank you, but I did really care about Carl and want justice for him. Even if it turns out that Gregor killed him."

"It's very odd that he would deliver an empty briefcase to him, which is then nowhere to be found. If the killer took it, wouldn't it mean that he had it in his possession?" I said. If I gave her the impression that I'm brainstorming with her, she might trust me enough to open up to me.

"Yes, unless he got rid of it."

"Why do that if it's his briefcase?"

"Good point."

I smiled. "Anyway, there's something else I need to discuss with you. Wendy said she overheard you talking about a lawsuit once. Is that related to Carl in any way? Otherwise I wouldn't ask, of course." I used my most non-threatening tone and hopefully gave her a look that told her she could tell me anything.

She sighed.

"A good sign," Detective Black said.

"It was because I had shared a story idea with Carl and then overheard him pitch that same idea to his own agent. I wanted information on what I could do if that happened, and a lawsuit was the only way. I was planning on threatening him with a lawsuit, but then I dropped it."

"Why?"

She looked down. "Because I respected him, and I could learn from him. I figured that instead of messing with his reputation, we could work together. We could share the credit and co-write instead. That way we could produce more books and make more money. He liked the idea."

Detective Black scoffed. "Of course he did. This meant he didn't have to come up with any ideas anytime soon."

"When did you decide this?"

"About two weeks ago. I've neared the end of my manuscript, but he won't be here to see it." She looked at her hands and briefly closed her eyes. "The only good thing that has come out of this whole mess is Eddie. He's so sweet." She smiled at the thought of him.

"Speaking of romance," I said. "Are you sure those bruises weren't caused by *someone* instead of *something*?"

She gave a rueful smile. "I realise the writer's mind is very imaginative, but I assure you I'm fine."

It still wasn't an answer to my question. "Wendy thinks you might have been running away from someone or something."

Sophia shook her head. "That doesn't surprise me. She is someone who always has a hidden agenda herself. Of course she assumes everyone else has them too. What I wanted more than anything was to connect with Carl and to write. At least I can still do one of those things." She tapped her laptop.

"Yes. Where would we be without our stories, right?"

Though her words reassured me, I left the park with a hint of worry. I could see what Wendy meant. Her words were sincere and Sophia portrayed something fragile and sweet, but there was also something about her that didn't quite match that image. Still, that didn't mean that Sophia was a liar or had something to hide. I knew someone who would always act helpless around men, just so they would underestimate her. It was a form of self-protection, one that perhaps Sophia used as well.

Our wounds from the past determined where we put up our armour in the present.

My mobile buzzed, and I had a message from Eleanor, asking me to come around to the vicarage. It was only three minutes away.

When I got there, Eleanor opened the door before I had a chance to ring the bell. She looked pale and let me in.

"Is everything okay?" I asked.

"Yes, I think so. I don't know." She hadn't blinked yet.

"You're scaring me."

She didn't reply and went into the kitchen. She stopped next to the breakfast table and pointed at it. On top of the round table was a brown leather briefcase. It was opened.

"Holy cupcakes," I said.

"Indeed."

I took a step closer. I had never seen this much money before. "How much do you think is in there?"

"I don't know. Do you think it's related to the murder?"

I glanced at her over my shoulder. "Oh, I know it is."

"Good heavens, I was afraid of that. I'll ring Alistair."

ALISTAIR SHOWED UP twenty minutes later. By that time, Eleanor had already drunk four cups of relaxing herbal tea. She was on the toilet when he rang the doorbell, and I answered.

"Any reason Eleanor contacted you before me?" Alistair said by way of greeting.

"She wasn't sure if it had anything to do with the murder." I waved him through to the kitchen where the briefcase had remained. Untouched.

Well, any more than it already had.

"Eleanor found it in the church's confessional booth."

Alistair leaned forward. "Ten thousand pounds," he said.

"Your Maths skills are impeccable," I said, impressed. Numbers had never been my friend.

Eleanor entered the kitchen. "Alistair, I'm so glad you came. I found this in the confessional booth. When I opened it, I nearly had a heart attack. I rang Maggie because I thought it could be related to that poor man's death. I didn't want to disturb you, in case it wasn't."

"Don't worry, I'm always available to help out." He gave her a warm smile. "I can understand it gave you a fright. It's not everyday you find a briefcase with that much money." He turned to me. "And to reply to your earlier comment: I know it's ten thousand pounds because that is what he withdrew from the bank the day of his death."

Eleanor and I exchanged a glance.

"So he was either blackmailing someone or he wanted to pay someone off. Do you think that it is related to what Gregor said? That he had knocked someone up?"

Alistair looked at Eleanor.

She made a zipping motion across her lips, then said: "I'll make you some tea. Go sit in the front room."

Alistair used a handkerchief to close the briefcase and then wrapped it around the handle, taking it with him. He was too careful to leave it out of his sight, even if we were only in the next room.

We sat down next to each other on the sofa. It had a floral pattern and was firm. The room itself was filled with several vases with wildflowers and a big clock hung over the fireplace.

"Do you think that Carl left it there? So he could retrieve it easily after whoever he was meeting showed up? Or did the killer put it there?"

Alistair sighed, and in this light he looked tired. "I don't know. We've been questioning Gregor but so far no results. I would feel so much better if he just confessed. And now with this briefcase...if Gregor was the killer, then wouldn't he have taken the briefcase with him? Or for that matter, why wouldn't the killer, regardless of who it was, *not* take that money?"

"I've been thinking the exact same thing, and the only reason I can think of is that the person was offended. If it was a woman he was bribing to get rid of their baby, then it could be that she wanted nothing to do with the money," I said.

"Yes, that's true. Wendy was acting quite obsessed. Perhaps he tried paying her off?"

I frowned. "I doubt he thought she was worth that kind of money just to be left alone. In fact, I think he enjoyed the attention. Also, I spoke with Sophia. Carl stole her story idea a few weeks ago, and she was getting ready to sue him, but then she decided to collaborate with him instead. I doubt it was hardly a collaboration, but more him sticking his name on the cover, but she said that's what they had decided on. I don't know if it's true. If she was planning a lawsuit then perhaps a lawyer can confirm it?"

"Yes, that should be easy enough to check out. I'll talk to her before I head back to the station."

"We know he had a habit of stealing stories and a habit of sleeping around with women. It seems likely that one of those things got him killed, but what if we are barking up the wrong tree?"

Alistair smiled wryly. "That's the whole problem with this case. There are so many suspects and motives, yet no proof."

"I can see how your job can be quite frustrating. Not only do you have to know, but you also have to be able to prove it."

Eleanor walked in with two cups of tea and biscuits. "Don't despair, dears. 'Let us not be weary in doing good, for we will reap in due season if we don't give up.'" She winked at me. "Sorry, I know you hate bible quotes, but I think this one fits the situation. You guys are doing remarkably well. You are working hard, you are not giving up. It will pay off, I promise."

"I admire your faith," I said, "and I hope you're right. I really don't want a murderer to get away."

"Don't worry. I'm like a Pitbull with a bone. I refuse to let go." Alistair smiled. "And right now we should be pleased that we have another clue. I'll have it checked for prints. Hopefully, we'll get something."

He hurriedly finished his tea and got up. "Thanks for the tea. I'll get going. No rest for the wicked."

Eleanor chuckled.

"I'll walk you out," I said.

"Thanks."

I walked him all the way to his Beetle in which he placed the briefcase.

"You have your dinner tonight, don't you? With Miles and his parents?" He sounded casual, but the tension in his jaw betrayed him.

"I do, yes."

His dark eyes searched my face. "Call me after."

"Why?"

"I just want to know how it went."

I grinned. "Are you jealous?"

"Not at all, don't be absurd." He touched his tie.

"Good."

"And how are things with Christina and you?"

"Actually, they are getting better. Thanks for asking." I smiled.

"I'm really glad to hear that." His eyes softened, and he bent down to kiss my cheek.

"Be careful. People might start talking."

"They probably already are." He winked and got in his car.

Detective Black cleared his throat. "Then I wonder what they would say about you meeting Miles' parents and being introduced to them as his girlfriend."

I winced inwardly. Yeah, that kind of gossip would follow me to my grave.

Chapter 17

I went back inside to finish my tea with Eleanor. I figured she could use the company while Harold was busy outside. He loved the feeling of helping his 'flock,' as he put it. Even if it was with something as minor as handing out healthy snacks and chatting with the tourists.

"Are you feeling better now?" I asked Eleanor.

She nodded and colour had returned to her round cheeks. "Yes, thank you, dear. I just can't imagine—do you really think Carl was being blackmailed or that he wanted to bribe someone?"

"I don't know yet. But that seems most likely."

She shook her head. "How tragic. First Victor was murdered and now this man. It's all rather upsetting, isn't it?"

"Yes, I agree." Especially finding him. There had been so much blood.

"How are you getting on with Alistair?" she asked, putting her porcelain tea cup to her lips. She avoided eye contact.

"Fine," I said, my voice high. Then I told her about what had happened with Christina and what Alistair had told me about his psychologist.

"I'm sure Christina will come around. She's just processing her relationship with Alistair. As for Alistair, well, I'm glad he's working on his happiness. It's very brave to admit that something isn't working, or that you're not happy. At least he's taking the proper steps."

"That is true." I hadn't thought of it as brave before, but I suppose she was right. Perhaps I should tell him that. It might mean a lot to him.

We chatted for a while, until the world seemed normal again, then I went on my way to the shop. I needed to brainstorm, and I needed post-its to do it. As I neared the Wicked Bookworm, Nancy left her shop with Gus. They were talking, their faces serious.

My heart sank. At least she would know, but it hardly made anything better.

I slipped into Nancy's shop to check on Emblyn. She was at the counter, drinking tea.

"Hey, look at you. Nancy already trusts you enough to run this place without her," I said with a smile.

Her eyes sparkled. "Do you really think so? I think it's just because someone came to take a walk with her, so she had no choice."

"There's always a choice. She trusts you. That means you've been doing well."

She beamed. "We have been chatting a lot. She's very strange, but I like her."

That pretty much summed up my aunt. "I'm glad."

"Also, I followed your advice and invited my dad to the wine tasting. He said it was a good idea."

"Excellent. See, you'll notice he'll start dancing to the slow rhythm of this village. Although, with all this murder and mayhem, the rhythm might be picking up."

"I think it's exciting. I mean, bad, obviously, but also exciting. Have you found out anything with your detective?" She wiggled her eyebrows.

"Hey, *I'm* your detective," Detective Black said.

"What has Nancy told you about Alistair?" I folded my arms.

"Not much."

I raised my eyebrow.

"Just that you want to marry him and have his babies." She laughed.

"Of course she did," I muttered. "Well, don't worry. Nobody is having babies anytime soon."

"I can't wait to have babies. I mean, I can, but I am so looking forward to it."

"You are? Aren't you scared?" I asked.

"Of what?"

"Of like...life and everything that comes with it? Don't you find it scary to fall in love? I mean, you'll either break up or you end up marrying the person. That's always pretty nerve-wracking to think about. Also, being pregnant and giving birth is no joke, not to mention motherhood."

"You can't hide in books all your life," Emblyn said with a smile. "It may be tempting, and it certainly would be easier, but it's also less fun."

"You're very smart, I should come to you for advice more often," I said.

"Don't be too quick to say that. The other day I mistook a dust bunny for a rat and shrieked my head off. Bailey went ballistic, thinking we were under siege, and Nancy nearly had a heart attack." She giggled.

"I'm so glad to hear you're becoming just as weird as the rest of us." I nudged her. "I'll see you later."

"Bye."

I went through the curtain behind the counter and emerged through it on the other side. Brian was behind the counter since Christina had the afternoon off.

"Hey, Brian, do you know where Christina is?" At that moment she walked in with the last bit of an ice cream cone. "Never mind," I said and hurried over. "Hey. I'm having dinner tonight with Miles and his parents. He wants me to be his pretend girlfriend, because his dad is giving him a hard time about dating. The thing is, I don't know what to wear. Will you help?"

"Give her puppy eyes, and she can't resist," Detective Black said.

I did.

"Sure, I'll help," she said and finished the rest of her ice cream.

"See?" Detective Black smiled at me.

Upstairs I gave Christina a fashion show with my favourite outfits. She liked all of them.

"What do you want your outfit to say?" she asked.

"Err. Nothing. It would be weird if clothes talked."

"Yes, utterly," Detective Black said.

She smirked. "No, I mean, what do you want your outfit to portray? The parents will judge you by your cover, so to speak. Do you want to look professional, casual, chic, creative? What?"

"Oh. I guess I want to look like a nice, reliable girlfriend."

She laughed. "That's the lamest answer I've ever heard."

"Hey!"

"All the outfits look nice on you. I think you should go with the one you are most comfortable with. That way you'll show them the real Maggie, and they can't help but love you."

I spontaneously teared up.

"Are you crying?" she asked.

"No, you're crying, shut up." Then I sat next to her on the bed and hugged her. She hugged me back.

"I've missed you," I said, sobbing.

"I've missed you too," she said and squeezed me tight.

I SPENT UNTIL FOUR o'clock writing, since I was first and foremost a writer and couldn't forget that. I had deadlines to make, and they were looming closer. Normally I had no problem with deadlines, but this murder was messing with my daily goal of finishing a chapter.

I changed into a floral dress with sandy coloured shoes with small heels. I liked the sound heels made when they clicked on the pavement or floor, but I disliked the torture high heels inflicted on my feet. Besides, it was also probably best to limit my opportunities to cause clumsy mayhem.

With a small handbag slung over my shoulder, I made my way downstairs. Christina was having fun in the village square, and she'd already wished me good luck. Despite the slight flutter of nerves I felt ready, and I was excited to be able to help Miles out. I couldn't imagine what it would be like if a parent hounded me to get a relationship. There were so many things that were beyond our control, and so the choices that we could make mattered. Miles had the right to choose whomever he liked to date, or not.

I closed the door behind me and had taken two steps before I recognised the figure at the back of Nancy's shop. He smiled at me.

"Alistair, what are you doing here?"

"Nothing. I was just in the neighbourhood."

I adjusted the strap of my handbag and walked over to him. "Is that so?"

"It is so." He put his hand on my lower back as we started walking. "But now that I'm here I might as well escort you to the Pembroke. Isn't that where you're heading? And why was that again?"

I glared at him. "To have dinner with Miles and his parents."

"Oh, right. Yes, of course. Dinner with Miles' parents because...what was the reason again? Something completely normal." He tapped his finger to his lips as he pretended to think.

"Because I'm pretending to be his girlfriend," I said as I rolled my eyes.

"Yep, that was it. An utterly sound reason."

"I don't like you when you're smug," I said.

He chuckled. "You either get Smug Alistair or Lecturer Alistair."

I made a face. "Then Smug Alistair it is."

"Are you nervous?"

"A little. You must have met his parents. Are they nice?"

"His mother is nice. His father was rarely there when I went over to play. Even when I stayed over, I didn't see him. He was always home late and gone early. I do know that he's quite controlling and arrogant. Quite the opposite of his mother. How they fell in love, I have no idea."

"Love works in mysterious ways," I said.

He eyed me. "You can say that again."

"Anything new with the case?"

"Gregor has gotten himself a lawyer. We had to let him go. All the evidence we have is circumstantial at best."

"I'm sorry. It's very frustrating, isn't it?"

"It is. But we'll worry about it tomorrow. First you have to wow your boyfriend's parents."

"That's right," I said as we walked on until we reached the Pembroke.

"What time will the parents arrive?"

I checked my watch. "In about two hours."

Alistair straightened. "And what are you going to do with Miles until they get here?"

"Why? What do you think we're going to do?"

He looked away and let out a long breath. "Fine, I know it's none of my business."

But I liked that he was acting as if it was. "Don't worry. We're not going to make passionate love, if that's what you're thinking. I came early so I can work on the library and have a drink with Miles before his parents arrive."

"Right. I am sure that you two will have a good time. Enjoy yourself." He cleared his throat and looked about as happy as an ice sculpture in the desert.

"You're welcome to come inside. You can help me with the books."

His eyes scanned my face for a moment. "No, no. It's alright. You've got to do what you've got to do."

"You're Miles' friend too, I'm sure he won't mind."

"No, you're the one he invited over. I don't want to act like a—well, never mind."

Detective Black scoffed. "Jealous boyfriend?"

"It's alright. I'll see you later then."

"Yes, later." He gave me a quick kiss on the cheek and dashed off.

"He's getting a bit kiss-happy, the sly bastard," Detective Black said.

I grinned and made my way up to the Pembroke and used the key to get in. "Miles?" I called out, then headed up to the library where I continued to work on the books. I did text him to let him know I was here already, figuring he was about somewhere.

A few minutes later he popped up in the library with a glass of red wine. He had rolled up his sleeves and undone his top buttons and was looking particularly handsome.

If you liked that sort of thing.

"I've started dinner preparations already. You look lovely."

I smiled as my cheeks felt warm. "Thanks. So do you. What are we having?"

"You'll see," he said. "Can I fetch you a glass as well?"

"No, thanks. I don't like wine."

"I'll be sure to remember that. Well, I'll leave you to it then. Be sure to be done in an hour, then we can relax a bit before my parents show up."

"Sure." I wanted to ask him how Kelly was, but I would save that for later. For now, I wanted to do something with my hands other than typing. I filled two whole boxes before my back was starting to get sore, and I was ready to head down. I picked up four more books from the row and then that would be done. One of the books got caught on something, and I lost grip on all of them. I tried catching them, but they fell to the ground. I carefully picked them up, praying I hadn't done irreparable damage.

"I think they're fine, but maybe you should check what they got stuck on. It couldn't have been the top of the shelf," Detective Black said.

I glanced at the shelf and ducked. My heart started beating faster. There was definitely something stuck to the top of that shelf. I put the books away and touched it. It was stuck with tape. With minor effort I wriggled it free. It was a USB flash drive.

"A new clue. Well done, Maggie."

"Thanks," I said to Detective Black and ran down. Miles was in the kitchen, on his iPad. The kitchen smelt lovely. He was clearly preparing some sort of soup, while ingredients for the main course were laid out on the counters.

I held up the newly uncovered clue. "I found this in the library. If my hunch is correct, Carl put it there."

At this, Miles perked up. "I'll get my laptop." A moment later he returned. "What do you think it is?" he asked as he put the laptop on the breakfast table.

"I'm not sure. It could be an audio file, mysterious emails, a manuscript." I had to stop talking or my imagination would take over and the list would never end.

Miles took the flash drive and stuck it in the laptop. "There's only one file. *Poised to Quill,* it's called." He opened it. "Oh, it's a manuscript. You're right."

"Just a lucky guess. But look at the name at the front page. It's Sophia's."

"Is this evidence, then?" He looked rather hopeful as he asked this.

"I wish. I already knew Carl was working on it with her. What I don't get is why he'd hide it in the library."

Miles stood up and put his hands in his pockets. "What makes you think they were working on it together?"

"She said so."

"That's not much proof then, is it. She could have been lying. She could have found out and killed him in a fit of rage."

Smart lawyer. "Yes, except that she had already phoned someone in order to get ready to sue him. But then she changed her mind. Wendy overheard her. Apparently they had agreed to put both their names on the story, start working together. I think she wanted some of his fame, and he wanted a good novel. There is no reason for him to hide the original manuscript. But what is weird is that she said he'd never read it. That she'd only pitched the idea." I checked the word count, then scrolled to the end. It was nearly finished by the looks of it. It stopped after the first few paragraphs of chapter 28.

"It does seem unlikely he was planning on stealing it still. Sophia would have sued him, not to mention that it would kick up a storm, since others were coming out of the woodwork."

I thought of Rachel. "True." I took the USB flash drive out of the laptop and tucked it into my handbag. "The plot seems to be thickening, doesn't it?"

"Isn't that a good thing?"

"For us, yes. For the murderer, no."

Chapter 18

Miles made sure the fire in the sitting room was burning, and we had a cheese platter out. There were now a leather sofa and a glass coffee table, with a set dining room table in the back. When the doorbell rang, I nearly spilled my grape juice.

"You'll be fine," Miles said. "It's me that will be in the hot seat tonight." He answered the door while I got up and waited by the sofa. His mother's feminine voice drifted over immediately. His father grumbled something.

I adjusted the skirt of my dress and smiled when his mum walked in. She beamed when she saw me, and she furtively looked me up and down.

"Nice to meet you, I'm Maggie Matthews," I said and held out my hand.

"Victoria," she said as she shook my hand. His mother looked like she came straight out of one of those fashion magazines. She wore an expensive-looking dress with a pearl necklace. Her blonde hair was cut right below her ears. She had a sincere smile that had the effect of immediately putting me at ease.

Miles' dad, however, had the opposite effect. He kept his hands in the trouser pockets of his tweed suit and regarded me with narrowed eyes. I felt like a prized poodle being judged for a competition.

"Dad, this is Maggie," Miles said, since he still hadn't introduced himself.

"Maggie, huh?" he said and stepped forward to shake my hand. It was one of those bone crunching handshakes, and though I did my best to return a firm handshake, it only made him squeeze my hand harder. I managed not to cringe.

"Rude," Detective Black said.

"Yes, that's me," I said.

"Rupert Mortimer." Then he regarded the snacks we'd laid out and the room we were in. "Bit odd of you to buy a hotel, son."

"Not odd at all. It's a gorgeous estate that I can easily transform into a lovely home." Miles managed to keep a cool tone, but I noticed the tension in his shoulders already.

"Please, sit," I said. "Miles cooked dinner. He's an excellent cook."

"Did he win you over with his cooking skills?" his mother asked.

"That was definitely a part of it." I smiled.

"Was the other part his bank account?" Rupert pricked an olive and popped it into his mouth.

"Darling," she warned.

"Relax, she knows I'm joking. It's all in good fun."

This was a whole new level of rude. Once I had a customer demanding to return a book that she'd clearly dropped into her bathtub, but that seemed like a walk in the park compared to this man.

Miles looked at me, and I smiled, letting him know it hadn't gotten to me. It had. Not for my sake, but for the sake of Miles and any future girlfriend he might have. His dad's behaviour was not acceptable, and the fact that both Miles and his mum responded so mildly meant that this was typical behaviour for the man. They had gotten used to it. I could just imagine his mother saying to Miles: 'Oh, you know how your dad is.' And just like that, a grown ass man got away with shitty behaviour.

"Now, Maggie," Victoria said, "tell me about yourself. Miles told us so little about you."

"I run the local bookshop, and I'm an author of a detective series."

"A successful detective series," Miles added. "You know them, Mum. It's the Detective Black series."

She gasped. "No way. I've read one of those books. I didn't realise that was you. It was a while back when I read it, and I'm terrible with names."

My cheeks warmed. "That's alright."

"You must not make a lot of money with it if you're still forced to work at your bookshop," Rupert said.

I curled my hands into fists.

"Dad, don't be rude. Besides, what does it matter how much she makes?"

His dad levelled him with a steely gaze.

"Actually," I said. "I am not forced to work at my bookshop. I run it and occasionally help out on the floor because I love it. And I suppose I need it as well. Though I make enough money with my books, I don't want to be cooped up in my office all the time, which is what would happen if it was my only job. This way I get to be around books, which I love, and people, which I also love."

"So, you have a double income," Rupert said, regarding me with a hint of respect for the first time.

"Yes, sir."

"Do you live in one of these cottages I've seen on the way over?"

"No, I live in the flat above my bookshop. Next to my aunt."

An alarm went off on Miles' phone. "That will be dinner," he said and jumped up. "If you would all sit at the table back there, I'll get the things from the kitchen."

"I'll help," I said and followed him, feeling myself relax more now that I was away from his awful father.

"Are you alright?" he asked me in the kitchen.

"Yeah, but I can't believe he actually speaks to people like that."

"I know. That is why I prefer to see as little as possible of the man," Miles said.

"I don't get it. You're so smart and capable, you're a sharp lawyer. How come you've never put him in his place? I'm just curious, I'm not judging."

He sighed and looked away. "I only stood up to him once, and he kicked me out of the house. I was nineteen and stayed with Alistair for two weeks before I returned home. We all pretended nothing had happened. I suppose I cared too much about what he thought of me. I guess because he's my dad."

"Family is overrated," I said. "Nobody asks to be born. And what family you are born into says nothing. It's just chance. Or fate, whatever you want to call it. But the point is, if family is so important, then why isn't he the one acting like it as well?" I had gone through a similar thing with my dad, and the moment I realised I could create my own family with the people who did truly care for me, a weight had been lifted.

Then again, I couldn't decide for Miles how important his dad was for him.

"Trust me, I've thought about this a lot, but there's no communicating with the man. It's his way or the highway, and unfortunately my mother is part of the package. Let's just get through this evening, and then you'll never have to see him again. I promise. Now, help me carry this."

First we carried out the potato soup, then he handed me the salad and rice while he carried the pan of curry. It was a special kind of curry with a secret ingredient, apparently, and it looked mouth-watering.

We sat down, toasted, and dug in.

The food barely made up for the company. Just barely.

WE WERE HALFWAY THROUGH dessert when things took a turn for the worse. It started off with an innocent enough question. His mother asked me if I had grown up here.

"My aunt took me in at a certain age, when things with my mother became worse. She had some mental problems," I explained.

Rupert leaned forward, towards his son, and said: "You know that most psychiatric disorders are hereditary, right?" He made a futile attempt to lower his voice, but I heard him. We all heard him.

I was holding my wine glass and gripped it so tightly that the stem broke. Blood dripped off my thumb.

"Dear heavens," Victoria uttered.

Miles pushed back his chair. "Come on, to the kitchen." He grabbed my arm and rushed me to the sink where he rinsed off the wound. He turned to grab a first-aid kit from one of the cupboards, and when he wanted to put a band-aid on the wound, he noticed my hand shaking.

He looked up.

I was crying silently.

"Damn it, damn it, damn it," Miles said with increasing volume. Then he kicked the cupboard between us, making me flinch. He legged it out of the room. I heard shouting.

"Apologise to her!" Miles said.

"I simply stated a fact," his dad shouted.

The sound of clattering dishes.

"You're not your mother. You're not crazy," Detective Black said, appearing in front of me.

The fact that *he* was telling me I wasn't crazy made me cry harder. I put my hand over my ears. "Stop talking to me. I want you to go away."

Detective Black looked wounded, and he took a step back, as if I'd slapped him.

"Go away," I said, sobbing. Then sat down on the floor, my legs drawn up to my chest.

Miles returned. "Maggie?" The cooking island was between us, so he couldn't see me. But he walked around it and found me on the floor. "Maggie, are you okay?" He sat down next to me and pulled me into him, holding me tightly as he kissed the top of my head. "It's okay. They're gone. I'm sorry. I'm so sorry."

I waited until the tears had dried and said: "I know something fun we can do." I refused to let this visit end on a bad note.

"READY?" I ASKED.

"Ready." Miles grinned.

I had changed into one of Miles' shirts, one that barely reached my knees. I also wore woollen socks. Per my instructions, Miles wore the same.

I'd created a long path from the dining table to the sofa with dish soap and water. Pillows were stacked up against the back of the sofa in case I'd fall.

I started running and then did a little hop, holding my arms out for balance. I slid across the floor on my soggy socks and made it halfway. "Damn it," I said. "Okay, you try."

He started sliding, but lost his balance and continued to slide on his belly.

"Oh, that looks like fun." I waited until Miles got up to add some more dish soap and water, using the plant spray.

This time I let myself fall onto my belly, which hurt, but at least I reached the pillows. "Yeah," I shouted in triumph.

Miles did some sort of battle cry, and I looked behind me. He was sliding towards me on his butt. I shrieked as he reached me, and he toppled over, right on top of me.

"Interesting development," a familiar voice said.

We both turned our heads to the shiny black shoes in front of us. Our gazes travelled upwards until we looked into Alistair's disapproving eyes.

"Hello, mate," Miles said.

"Problem, officer?" I giggled.

Miles got up and pulled me to my feet as well.

"What happened? I saw your parents at the pub. Your dad had a bruise on the side of his face," Alistair said.

I glanced at Miles. He hadn't told me that.

Miles just shrugged. "He said something stupid. Anyway, want some leftover curry?"

Alistair observed my outfit. "Why are you wearing Miles' shirt?" His voice was tense.

"This is what you should wear when you go sliding through your home. Besides, otherwise my dress would get dirty."

"Oh, but it doesn't matter if my shirt gets dirty?" Miles asked, pretending to be insulted.

"I could hardly go in my underwear, could I?"

"Yes, she could hardly go in her underwear, could she?" Alistair said.

Miles chuckled. "It's the same as a bikini. Now, are you going to take off your trousers and join us?"

"Yeah, Alistair. Are you going to take off your trousers?" I said.

Miles and I spent the next twenty minutes sliding over the floor while Alistair had taken out a stopwatch to time our personal records. He also was on dish soap and water duty and took this very seriously. The one time that Miles had started sliding before Alistair was ready, he sprayed Miles in the face with the water spray.

My stomach hurt from laughing, and I was covered in dish soap from head to toe. "Okay, I really need to clean up. Do you have a towel for me?"

"Actually, you can use the guest bedroom for personal guests. Go past the kitchen, on the right."

"Okay, thanks." I hurried off to the room he was talking about. It was next to Mr Field's former burnt-down office. Miles had made two rooms out of it, the other half clearly still under construction. I made half a towel wet and got rid of most of the soap, then I dried myself. I'd definitely have to take a shower as soon as I got home.

I hadn't seen Detective Black since I told him to go away, but right now I needed to ruminate. Technically Rupert had simply mentioned a fact, but it had opened up a trapdoor in my mind that I preferred to keep closed.

When I returned to the men, they were chatting quietly at the dining table. Miles was wet and soapy, Alistair looked crisp as ever. He got up when he saw me. "I'll walk you home, if that's okay," he said.

"Sure. Thanks. Miles, I'll see you around."

Miles got up and kissed me on the cheek. "I'll make it up to you," he whispered in my ear, and then kissed me again.

I smiled. "You know, as someone who knows how much families can suck, here's what I've learned: you can make your own family."

"Yes, I took Biology classes," he said with a cheeky grin.

"No, I mean, you can find people who—"

"I know what you mean, love. You are a beautiful person, and don't you forget it." He tapped my chin.

"Stop it," I said as I felt myself getting shy. I nudged him, but he lost his balance and nearly fell.

Alistair chuckled. "It must be because you're so slippery."

Miles looked down at himself. "Yes, I'm fairly sure I could simply slide to the grocery store if I wanted to."

I laughed at the image.

We left after a final goodbye and ventured into the cooler night air. I couldn't wait to be in my air-conditioned flat. Alistair walked alongside me in silence. Judging by the frown etched between his eyebrows, Miles must have told him what had transpired earlier. I wasn't sure how I felt about that, but I couldn't blame Miles for telling him.

I felt embarrassed for breaking down like that. One poke at my sore spot, and I fell apart. But I suppose I had nothing to feel bad about. There was nothing wrong with crying, right? Yet, somehow I was always embarrassed by it. Even when I cried in front of Nancy or Eddie.

Alistair walked me back to my flat. "Will you be alright?"

"Of course," I said in my usual chipper voice.

He narrowed his eyes at me and opened his mouth to say something, then shut it again. "Good night, then." This time he hugged me. It was a long hug. I needed it.

When I was up in my flat, I got a text message and checked it. It was from Alistair.

There is nothing wrong with you. In fact, everything is right with you. Xxx

I smiled.

Chapter 19

That Saturday morning I woke up early to help Alistair with the scavenger hunt. I was looking forward to it. Every hour starting from noon till four, we'd take small groups to find the clues and help them. Most of them were in the woods, and we made sure to give them hints if needed. It would not be fun if they didn't succeed, much like with a murder investigation. I was going to go to Alistair's early, so we could set up the treasure chest and put the clues in place.

Christina was still sleeping when I had my breakfast, and I contemplated making her breakfast in bed, but it was very possible that she didn't like being woken. Even if it was for food. So instead, I bounced downstairs and went around to Nancy's flat. She was wearing fuzzy slippers and a pink robe that assaulted my eyes. "Tea?" she asked without looking up.

"Nah, already had some," I said.

"So, how was dinner with the in-laws? Did you have to fake an emergency and run? Did you have to stab someone with your fork?" She chuckled.

"Just because you once emptied a vase with roses and all on your date's mother, doesn't mean I did."

"She had it coming," Nancy said.

"So you were always this violent, huh?"

She shrugged. "I prefer temperamental."

"I'm sure you do." I picked up Bailey from the floor and snuggled him. He wagged his tail and tried to lick my ear.

"You still haven't answered the question. Don't make me hear it through the grapevine." She popped two pieces of toast in the toaster.

She would definitely hear about the bruise on Rupert's face, but I couldn't tell her the truth. I simply couldn't repeat what that man had said. So instead I said: "Rupert, Miles' dad, slipped on some dish soap and hit his face. But I'd appreciate it if you made the story a bit more exciting when you put it through the rumour mill. You know, the way you do with your eye."

She batted her eyelids at me. "Whatever do you mean?"

"Please. Christina said you told her you lost your eye in a hoover accident."

"So?"

"You told Emblyn you lost it playing golf. Besides, what do you mean 'so'? Christina was afraid to hoover for weeks. She had nightmares."

Nancy cackled with laughter.

"It's your turn now," I said. "What happened with Gus? I saw you two walking and talking."

She pressed her lips together. "We decided it's best if we go our separate ways."

I cocked an eyebrow. "Really? Is that what you want?"

"It's for the best. We've decided."

The toast popped up, and she turned her back to me.

"Okay, that's fine. Whatever you want, I support your decision. As long as you don't regret it. Though I suppose we can't look into the future and know what we'll regret. Life would be so much easier if we could."

She cleared her throat. "Are you helping Alistair with the scavenger hunt today?"

"Yep. About to head over and set things up."

"It's supposed to be two degrees cooler today," Nancy said. "Still hot, though. But then again, maybe Alistair will be so hot he takes his shirt off."

"Nancy!"

"What? I'm just saying, wouldn't hurt anybody if he did."

"I think Poppy would get a heart attack."

"What a way to go, eh?" She laughed again.

I couldn't help but laugh as well. "Fine, I'm leaving now, before you get worse."

"I'm always worse," Nancy shouted after me.

I GASPED IN SHOCK AS Alistair opened his front door.

"What?" he asked.

"You're wearing a t-shirt. And jeans." My jaw had dropped so hard, it reached middle earth.

"Yes, well, we'll be in the woods for the most part. What did you expect me to wear?"

"Your suit. I'm pretty sure you sleep in it."

He smirked. "No, I sleep naked."

Great. Now there was a heatwave taking place inside my body.

Alistair chuckled at my expression. "I like messing with you."

"Oh, no no. You can't take it back now. I'm still picturing it. Hang on."

"No, don't picture anything," he stepped forward and placed his hands over my eyes, as if that would help. "You'll just make me look more attractive than I am, and you'll set yourself up for disappointment."

I jumped back out of his reach and pointed at him. "Excuse me, sir, but what makes you think I'll see you naked at some point, huh?"

"I do beg your pardon, milady." He stepped forward. "But you know, just in case."

"Well, don't get your hopes up." I adjusted my skirt. "Let's go get the treasure chest." Before I would explode into a fireball.

We carried the treasure chest with fake gold and diamonds to the vicarage where Harold was already waiting for us. He waved. "Do you need me to help carry that?" he said with a mischievous grin.

"No, please, don't get up," I said, which elicited a chortle from Harold.

He had a table set up at the side of the vicarage, on the path that led into the woods. On it were sign-up sheets for the treasure hunt as well as lots of lemonade and paper cups. The starting clues were also laid out on the table. The bag with the other clues was on the ground next to Harold. It was dangerously close to tilting over against his wheelchair wheel.

We set down the chest and took a breather while Eleanor came out of the vicarage with two bottles of water. "I've brought these for you, guys. I'll put them on the table. Just let me know when you need more. I'll be around all day. I'm so excited for the scavenger hunt. Last year the kids were so eager to solve the brain teasers."

"I'm curious to see how many kids will sign up," Alistair said.

"Don't worry about that. There are always kids eager to join. Sometimes adults too. They say they do it for the kids, but really they like to try to solve the clues themselves. Last year Maggie invented the clues as well, and after the first round there were more and more adults joining."

I bit my lip. "Which is why I made them easier this time."

"It wasn't a bad thing," Harold said. "They wanted to join because the clues were so good."

"I can understand that. This year they're also very good," Alistair said as he smiled at me.

"Thanks."

We chatted for a bit and then went into the woods to hide the treasure chest. I covered it with some branches, but it was still visible. The kids would be so excited.

"This is going to be so much fun," I said.

"Yes, and hot. I'm already sweating, and it's still early."

"Don't worry. It will only get worse."

Alistair grumbled something.

When we returned, Eleanor had set up two plastic chairs for us so we could sit and wait in-between groups. First, we joined Eleanor and Harold in their back garden for iced tea. Then Eleanor helped us hang up and bury the other clues. It was about ten thirty when we wrapped things up.

I went to the shop to get some sweets for the kids for afterwards. As I approached the vicarage again, I was curious to see if a first group had already assembled.

It had.

"Oh, boy," I muttered. "What are you doing here?" I asked the women of the Castlefield Book Club. Poppy, Lily, Ava, Nancy, Phoebe, Jessica, and even Olivia and Nancy were there. They had on beach hats and large sunglasses.

Ava was rubbing sunblock like nobody's business. She was completely white. "If we can decipher your clues, lass, we might consider ourselves regular sleuths, just like you. We have to prove our worth, you know, if we want to keep helping you with these murders."

"Why do you say that like there will be more?" I asked.

"Knowing your gift for sniffing out crime, I'm sure there will be."

I made a face. I'd rather have a different gift. Maybe another baby bunny.

"Don't you think you should let the children go first?" I said.

"What children?" Lily asked. "There are no children yet. They are all sleeping in. We are your first group. Deal with it."

"I will deal with it. I will deal with it by shoving these clues so far up your—"

"Now, now," Alistair started, "we would be honoured to lead you lovely ladies to the bountiful treasure chest."

The women visibly swooned.

"Yes, yes, Detective Charming, just give us the first clue," Nancy said.

"Is the prize sweets?" Poppy asked, grabbing several sweets from the bowl reserved for the children. She then grabbed a second handful and stuffed the sweets in her shirt.

"No, the prize is a treasure chest," Ava said loudly in her ear. "He just said that."

"Alright, I'm not deaf. I just really want it to be sweets."

Eleanor, who had watched the whole exchange with interest, said: "I'll go fetch some more sweets, then. Just for you."

Poppy lit up like a spaceship.

"Alright," I said, checking my watch. It was nearly noon. "Let's start then. Welcome to the scavenger hunt, young—err, yeah, young sleuths. We will begin our adventure with the following clue." I rolled out the scroll with the riddle.

"Go towards the leafy giants, follow the red birds. When you come upon the rock, find the thing most out of the ordinary."

The women all started chatting at once. Normally I could follow them, but this time I could only make out snippets here and there.

"Woods."

"Painted wings."

"Idiot."

"Dividend tax rates."

"Okay," Nancy shouted above the cackle of women. "Let's all go forward since obviously we first have to go into the woods. Those are the 'leafy giants', unless it refers to tall weird people, but the only people that are weird here are us, and we're not tall."

"Huh?" Poppy asked.

"Leafy also means weird," I explained.

"Leaves aren't weird. They're natural," she said.

Everybody grunted.

Before a fight erupted, I stepped aside and let them all get on with it. I exchanged a glance with Alistair. "Remember how we thought this was going to be fun?"

He patted me on the back. "Don't worry. We'll get through this. How bad can it be?"

"MY FEET HURT, I THINK I'm dying from heatstroke," Poppy said after we had walked a total of two minutes.

"Don't worry," Ava said, "the only thing you might die of is strangulation. No offence, Alistair."

Alistair was clearly starting to loosen up around us since all he did was chuckle.

"Look, Angry Birds," Olivia said as she pointed at a low branch in one of the nearest trees. It was a stuffed animal from the game that Alistair had coiled around the tree with a wire.

"It's red. And there's another one," Phoebe exclaimed.

"We must follow them, hurry," Jessica said.

"They're hardly going to fly away, are they?" Ava laughed.

We all ignored that and followed the trail until we reached a small clearing where a picture of Dwayne Johnson was stapled to the trunk of one of the trees.

"Who is that?" Olivia asked and was the first to reach the picture.

"That's Dwayne Johnson, an actor. He played in a film about scorpions or something. And he looks angry a lot," Ava said.

"Isn't his nickname The Rock?" said Phoebe.

"Then we must find the thing that's most out of the ordinary," Olivia said.

Everyone started looking about, searching feverishly. They looked at the ground, checked around the nearest trees. Just when Phoebe had pushed Jessica up a tree to check something out, Poppy said: "Isn't the picture the thing that's most out of the ordinary?"

They all stopped.

Alistair and I exchanged a smile.

Poppy took the picture and turned it around. "Look, it's a treasure map."

"Oh, let me see," Phoebe said, and let Jessica go. She fell out of the tree with a thud.

"I'm okay," she grunted.

This time there were no complaints as the women eagerly followed the directions on the map. In fact, Poppy was the fastest of us all, and since she had the map, we struggled to keep up with her.

The map led us all to a challenge. There were a bunch of pictures of people striking silly poses that they had to strike as well, and only then did Alistair give them the next clue. He told them he would ask four trivia questions that were easy enough to answer. Then the first letters formed the direction in which they had to go next. The trees were marked with the four directions of a compass.

"The first question. What is the country with the most red phone booths?" he asked.

"Paris!" Poppy said. "No, wait, England. Sorry, nerves make me blurt out things."

"Right, England, very good," Alistair said.

"Do you need another question?" I asked.

The women all looked at each other. "Of course, you said there were four, go on."

Alistair and I exchanged a look.

"A blank a day keeps the doctor away," Alistair said.

"What's a blank?" Poppy asked.

"Apple," Olivia said.

"Very good."

"Okay, next question," Ava said. "We're on a roll."

"Are you sure you need the next question? You get four questions, each first letter of the answer representing the letters of the direction you're supposed to go in."

"Yes, we heard you. Hurry up," Poppy said.

I grunted. "You have four very different directions in which to go, remember? The first letters of the answer represent a four-letter word."

"Shit!" Poppy said happily.

A pause. Alistair started laughing.

Poppy started reciting more four-letter words, which only made Alistair laugh harder. Any longer and he'd be pissing himself.

"Oh, I get it," Nancy said. "We could have known after the first answer because only one direction starts with an 'e.'"

"Aaaah," all the women said.

Alistair was still laughing.

"At least you're having fun," I said to him.

We had two more riddles and one more challenge before the women finally found the treasure chest. We handed them all pouches so they could fill them up with the treasure, because that's what we'd do for the kids, but everyone except Poppy declined.

She showed me the bag with a proud smile. "Now, how many sweets can I buy with this?"

Chapter 20

At four o'clock we took down all the clues and returned the treasure chest, which took us nearly two hours. All Alistair and I really wanted was a nice unhealthy pub meal, and so we went to The Rose and both ordered cheesy chips and gravy. It always made me feel like I'd gained twenty pounds directly after the meal, but it was worth it.

"I'm glad there were plenty of kids who showed up. And worried that all of them were better than the Castlefield Book Club," I said. Callum had just brought our meals, and it was too hot to eat. The torture of having a deliciously smelling meal and not being able to eat it.

"Poppy really is something," he said and started chuckling at the memory.

"You're good with kids," I said.

"Thanks. I've always liked kids. You're good with them too, by the way. You were very sweet and encouraging."

I looked down at my plate. "Thanks."

"Do you want kids?" he asked.

"Yes," I automatically said, then remembered Rupert's words. "No. Maybe. I don't know."

"Why not?" He looked at me with patience, not revealing any sort of emotions on his face. No judgement.

I shrugged. "Just—I mean, it's really selfish, isn't it? What if you have kids and there's something—I mean, what if they have something bad?" I frowned and poked the cheesy chips with my fork.

"Maggie," Alistair said and put his hand over mine, "don't let other people tell you who you are."

"But what if those people are right?" I swallowed as I started to sweat.

He squeezed my hand. "Have you ever hurt yourself deliberately?"

"No, of course not," I said.

"Hurt anyone else deliberately?"

"No!"

"Then what's the problem?" He let go of my hand and took a bite of his chips. "This is delicious. But hot." He took several swigs of his pint.

Was it really that simple? No harm, no foul. I mean, Detective Black had always helped me. He showed up when I needed someone to talk to, or to crack a joke, or when I started to panic about something. So, did it really matter if he was my imagination or not?

I felt tears in my eyes as a huge weight started to lift and ate my chips with blurred eyes, while Alistair pretended not to notice.

It was lovely.

AFTER DINNER WE TOOK a walk and ended up at the Antique Shoppe. The light was still on in the back.

"Do you mind if we go in?" I said. "I want to make sure he's okay. My aunt told me that they'd had a chat and decided to stay separated. I feel bad for him. He's all alone, and he's doing it to protect Nancy."

"I'm sorry to hear that, but I understand. It's not something that should be taken lightly."

"Yes, and he's very brave for doing this. They both are, so I want to help in any way I can."

Alistair touched my cheek. "Then that's what we'll do."

I knocked on the door.

Again Gus came shuffling out of the back room. He froze for a moment as he observed us, then hurried to the door and unlocked it for us. "What brings you here? Is your aunt okay?"

"Yes, she's keeping busy. We just wanted to make sure you were doing alright."

He turned the lights on in the shop. "There, now we can see what we're saying."

I chuckled. "Thanks. So, how are you doing?"

"I guess I'm alright. I think it was the right decision. Loss is the most painful feeling, nothing can truly heal it. I really don't want to do that to your aunt."

I wanted to say that she'd experience it anyway, but decided to keep that to myself.

"Do you have anyone to look after you for when things—get worse?" Alistair asked.

"I've asked my nephew to stay with me for a while when that happens, but so far so good. I plan on doing as much as I can myself."

"And are you doing anything special in the months that you're still okay?" I asked.

He laughed. "You mean the infamous bucket list? Oh, no, those things are nonsense. People should not make lists for things they want to do once they realise they're dying. We're dying from the moment we are born. I've done all the things I've wanted to do. I will simply enjoy my time here. This antique shop is my passion. You must understand as a shop owner," he said to me. "This place was first a shoe shop. I bought it quite cheaply, you know? And I was so excited to start. I had already collected a lot of antique items." He laughed again.

"When I first started, I found it so difficult to part with the items that I made them too expensive. But people bought them anyway. It hurt at first, but then I started to love it. Being able to watch people so happy with their new purchase. Giving an old object new life. It was thrilling. Not to mention that I always discover something new. I fill my shops with all sorts of new items."

Alistair started looking around the shop. "You do have some really nice things. I can't believe I've never looked around before."

I hadn't either.

"Well, you're always welcome."

"Thank you," Alistair said. "My dad used to collect—" his voice trailed off. "Err, Gus, how long have you had this?"

"What?"

Alistair had taken a handkerchief and was holding up the statuette of the quill. The murder weapon.

"Blimey," Gus said.

GUS GOT ALISTAIR A large zip-lock bag for the statuette. There was blood on it as well as a blond hair.

"Can you think of anyone who could have done this?" Alistair asked.

"I've been on the market every day except for today. You'll have to ask Breanna, she's worked here the last few days." He scratched his head. "I can't believe I haven't noticed."

I looked around the cluttered shop. I could.

"I need to make a few phone calls. Can you ring Breanna? Ask her to come in?"

"Of course, whatever you need." Gus hurried off.

"Sorry, Maggie. Can you get home okay?" Alistair asked.

"Yes. Just keep me updated, and let me know if I can do anything. I'll keep my phone on."

"Thanks."

I went back home where Christina was flicking channels on TV. She looked up. Snowball was on the ground, relaxing.

"Hey, how are you?"

"You won't believe what just happened." I sat down next to her and told her about how we found the murder weapon in Gus' shop.

"The audacity of the killer to just put it there," she said.

"Which also means that the blond hair is probably a setup. First I thought that the murder has been an opportunity, a-spur-of-the-moment decision. You know, perhaps an argument that got out of hand, with the pen in his chest as an afterthought. But now I think it might have been more calculated than that. What if the killer had planned it like this all along?" I shivered.

"Then it must have been someone who really didn't like him."

"Which is a long list of people. Even I didn't like him."

Christina nodded. "He was a sleazeball."

"A rapscallion."

"A scallywag."

We giggled, then turned serious.

"What will happen now?" she asked.

"They'll test it for prints and DNA. My guess is that there's nothing of the killer on there, but we'll see."

"Do you think you'll solve the case? You and Alistair, I mean?"

"I hope so, but this one isn't easy." I yawned. "What did you do today?"

"Mostly did some chores and reading. What's tomorrow?"

"Bowls and hula hooping," I said.

She made a face. "I think I'll skip that one."

"It's actually surprisingly fun, especially when you make up your own rules. And with the hula hooping, it's fun to watch. Especially when Eddie does it. He's very good. His hips have lives of their own, I tell you."

She laughed. "I'll make sure I see that. And take photographic evidence."

"Good. I'm going to write a bit and then go to bed. I'm sleepy."

"Okay, sleep well."

I gave Snowball a cuddle and stepped into my office. I started up my laptop and sighed. "I'm sorry, Detective Black. I didn't mean to yell at you. Please, come back."

I closed my eyes. When I opened them, he still wasn't there.

"Damn it." I opened the file of my latest project and started writing. I wrote for about twenty minutes and then hit a snag.

"What would be better? Have her lie or tell the truth," I muttered to myself.

"Have her lie," Detective Black said from behind me.

I whirled my desk chair around and got up to hug him. "I'm so glad you're back."

He blushed. "Yes, well, just get to work, young lady. We don't have all day."

I finished the scene and even wrote another one, after which I felt like it had been a successful day. I hopped under the shower and went to bed, when I realised I had intended to read Sophia's manuscript. I was too curious and retrieved my laptop as I settled in bed. I stuck the flash drive in my laptop and started reading the first chapter. Before long I'd read the first three.

I was surprised by how well she could write. She hadn't even needed Carl. She was skilful enough. So far the story was about a woman who went to meet someone she already knew, but apparently he didn't recognise her. She had created suspense and mystery and all that without even having a crime committed.

Though I was tempted to keep on reading, my eyelids were protesting, and I switched off the laptop. I dreamt about a treasure chest filled with scones.

THE NEXT MORNING I woke up at ten o'clock. I checked my messages as I remembered the events from last night. Alistair had sent me a message that he'd stop by in the morning.

I panicked as I checked the time and wanted to jump out of bed. My foot got caught on the duvet, and I fell flat on my face. Pain echoed through my body.

Footfalls sounded closer and closer until the door swung open and Christina surveyed the damage. "She's fine," she yelled.

"Who are you talking to?"

"Alistair. I was making him a drink and was about to wake you."

I ungracefully got to my feet. "Are you okay?"

"Yeah, I'm fine. Really. Take your time, we both know what you're like when you rush things."

I gave her an innocent smile. "Yes, ma'am."

When I entered the living room, Alistair was holding Snowball. He stroked her very gently while muttering sweet things to her. She seemed to enjoy it and had her eyes closed.

Christina was in the armchair, looking at them both with a smile on her face. "She's the softest, isn't she?" she asked.

"Yes, she really is," he replied.

"You wouldn't expect such a cute creature to poop as much as she does," I said.

They both looked up.

"Hello, Sleeping Beauty," Alistair said, then realised what he'd said and eyed Christina.

She just laughed. "I'll leave you two to it."

"You're welcome to stay," I said.

"No, I've got plans in the village. You guys have fun catching dangerous killers." She winked at me.

She seemed surprisingly okay with everything, which I admired about her. Her conversation with Alistair, and me, must have helped. Difficult things—even painful things—could still be good things.

I joined Alistair on the sofa. "Did you find out anything useful?"

"Yes. The hair belongs to Wendy. It could have fallen off her head as she plunged the knife in. We picked her up this morning, but she lawyered up. We have the right to hold her for a while, so maybe that will loosen her tongue."

"But?"

"But why place a bloody murder weapon in a shop, where it will be discovered? Unless you're not the killer and you want it found, because it proves someone else did it."

I snapped my fingers. "Exactly. That's what I was thinking. But if you know that, then why did you arrest her?"

"It will make the killer think he's safe. We want that. Right now, the killer seems to be one step ahead of us. Always. It's time to turn the tables on him."

"Good thinking. But like you said, we only have a few hours before we even have to let Wendy go," I said.

"I know, so we have to get some new clues fast."

"If only this were a story," Detective Black said. "Things would be so much easier."

Chapter 21

"Doesn't the fact that Wendy's hair is on the statuette mean that she didn't do it? I mean, if the killer wants to place the blame on someone else?"

"Yes. Unless it's a double bluff. But that's risky," Alistair said.

"It does indicate that someone didn't panic after killing him. It's possible that the killer planned this."

Alistair rubbed his face. "But we still don't know why, or who."

"Yeah, those questions are kind of important."

"Then there's also the possibility that it was someone who simply came here to kill him and then left."

I bit my lip. "It is possible that someone knew he would be here."

"Anyway, we'll just have to wait and see. Keep our eyes and ears open." He got up. "I better get back to work. I'll keep you updated if anything changes."

"Thanks. I'll do the same."

"Just be careful."

I gave him a smile. "Always."

After Alistair left I wrote for about an hour and then went to Nancy's shop to hang out. I hadn't expected Emblyn to be there since it was a Sunday, and she might have wanted to relax, but she was clearly dedicated.

I waited until Nancy was done selling incense to a few tourists, and then I told her about the murder weapon being found at Gus'. She'd already heard about it, because gossip spread fast, but she hadn't heard the details. Emblyn was listening while she was restocking the candles.

"And why were you at Gus'?" Nancy asked with narrowed eyes.

"I wanted to see how he was doing. I figured he was a tad lonely, perhaps. Or upset."

Nancy lowered her voice. "Was he?"

"He was putting on a brave face, I think. He was quite down to earth about it all, but he must miss you."

Nancy's lips turned downwards. "Yeah, well, I miss him too. But this is for the best. We haven't been together long, and taking care of someone in their final days is no small task."

"I don't think he's looking for a nurse. In fact, he's still fine enough, physically speaking. All he wants to do is work in his shop. You could easily go for a pub meal once a week or something. That might just be the thing both of you need," I said.

She tilted her head, her big hair unmoving as she did. "Hmm," she simply said, which meant that she would consider it.

At that moment, Sophia came in. "Ah, there you are," she said to me. "I heard about the murder weapon being found and Wendy being arrested. What a dreadful mess. First Gregor, now Wendy. I don't understand it at all. Do you think they were in on it together?"

Detective Black said, "They'd have to be very good actors if they were."

"I doubt it," I said. "But I also don't think Wendy did it."

Sophia nodded. "Because the murder weapon was placed in the shop by the killer. That is weird, isn't it?"

"Exactly. Especially when there's evidence on it."

"Unless the killer wants you to think that. I mean, if it was Wendy, then it means she could have been planning to cast suspicion on herself, only to have it cast on someone else later. Usually when someone's ruled out, they're not ruled back in," Sophia said.

She really, just like me, had a mystery author's mind.

"Yes, but it seems unlikely. Evidence is more important than hunches. She would have to be very sure that there's other evidence. Or a confession."

"So, do you need any help with anything? I've been a bit distracted by work and by Eddie, but I'm still willing to help, if you need it. I mean, I've finished my novel, and I'm itching to do something."

"Do you think it's possible that someone had an axe to grind and followed you guys here, with the intent to get rid of Carl? Was he ever threatened?"

"Only by that Rachel woman. Nobody else."

"Right."

"Do you think she set up a plan of some sort?"

"We know too little to know for sure," I said. "But if I do think of something you can help with so we can change that, I'll let you know."

"Thanks. I know Carl wasn't the nicest person, but I do hope there will be justice for him soon. I liked him."

I simply smiled.

When she left, Emblyn stepped away from the shelf with all the candles. "I recognise that woman," she said. "I think she was talking to our former cleaning lady once."

"Okay. Why is that special?" I asked.

"It wasn't, just a bit odd that they met up so late at night, that's all."

"Couldn't they have been friends hanging out?"

"It looked like they were arguing about something. Anyway, I don't know her very well. She cleaned for us once before she took up a new job at the hotel."

"Wait, wait, wait," I said. "Is your former cleaning lady Kelly?"

"Yeah, that was her name. She seemed nice, but apparently the new owner at the hotel paid her more." She shrugged. "Can't say I blame her."

"Do you know where she lives?"

"In one of those terraced houses behind the vicarage."

"She lives near the church?"

"I suppose." Emblyn frowned. "Why are you asking me all this?"

I looked at Nancy.

She nodded her head. "Go."

I dashed off.

"Is she always this weird?" I heard Emblyn ask.

"Yes," said Nancy loud enough for me to still hear.

KELLY'S SMALL FRONT garden was littered with gnomes. Most of them were nearly completely white because of the sun damage. I had texted Miles to ask for her house number, so I was sure I had the right place.

She opened the door after a minute. "It's you," she said with wide eyes. She looked around to see if I was alone. Maybe she was expecting Alistair. Was that because she had done something wrong? Was it risky for me to go in? I sized her up. I could probably take her in a fight.

"Of course you could," Detective Black said.

"Come in," she said and led the way to the kitchen where she was making some tea. "Do you want a cup?"

"Sure." I figured if I pretended this was a social call, I could make this easier. Hopefully she'd lower her guard.

She gave me a cup with too much milk and sugar, but I took it anyway. She was clearly accustomed to living alone and not having to ask anyone how they wanted their tea.

"So what brings you here? I heard about Wendy's arrest."

"I'm sure you did. The police are hoping to get a confession. How are you feeling about it?" I asked.

"It's terrible, of course. I mean, that it happened. I don't know, I just want this whole thing to be over with."

Her hand trembled slightly as she put her cup to her lips.

"Have you ever met the other authors? Did Carl ever introduce you to them?"

She shook her head. "No, not at all. I think he wanted as little to do with me as possible, in hindsight. I mean, I think deep down he had a good heart, but—"

"It didn't really show?"

She blushed. "I don't want to speak ill of the dead."

"Right," Detective Black said.

"Do you know anything at all about the other authors? Can you imagine any of them killing him?"

She looked at me. "I can't imagine anyone doing it. Nor do I want to go around thinking about murder, do I?" Then she remembered who she was talking to. "No offence."

I smiled. "None taken." Though I wasn't sure what to discuss next, I wanted some more time to chat with her. Get her to soften up a bit, before I would bring up Sophia.

"I grew up in Birmingham," she said. "When I was little, I visited one of our neighbours. She was very sweet and always left her front door open. She also always had biscuits that she'd give to the kids. Sometimes I'd just go over to have some milk and biscuits, and she'd talk with me about my day. The dad would come home, and we'd all sit there like a proper family. It was nice."

"That does sound nice."

"But one time I went over there and there was red stuff on the carpet. I thought for a minute she had spilled some juice, but it smelt funny, and I knew something was wrong." She started tearing up. "It turned out that someone had come in and robbed her, then killed her when she put up a fight." She cried.

I put my hand on hers, and she smiled appreciatively.

"I'm sorry, I don't know why I'm telling you this. It's just awful what people do to each other, isn't it?"

"It is," I said.

She got up to blow her nose and when she calmed down, I got ready to ask her. "Sophia is one of the authors. Someone saw you and her arguing together. Which means that you do know her." If I said it as if I was already a hundred percent sure, it would make it harder for her to lie.

She started crying again and nodded. "Yes."

"I have to know. What from? What were you arguing about?"

She shook her head and continued crying. It took a while, and all that time I sat there patiently until she softly told me to go.

"What?"

"I won't tell anyone anything except for the police," she said with conviction.

"So there is something to tell."

"Please, leave. Now." She looked at me with determination, but the corner of her mouth twitched.

Still, I didn't mind whether or not she told me. As long as she told the police.

"Alright, then." I got up and left. I closed the door behind me, relieved she hadn't stabbed me in the back while I'd walked out. I mean, you never know. It would be just the kind of danger I'd love to put Detective Black in.

"Yes, just typical. Always putting me in danger right after the reveal," he said. "It's getting old."

"Putting your protagonist in danger never gets old," I said. Just as I took out my phone to ring Alistair, Pandora crossed the street and our eyes met. For a second I was frozen. Surely she would not attack me. We had an understanding. *I think.*

She let out one of her infamous screeches, and I ran, going straight towards the church. I'd hide at Eleanor's. I glanced behind me as I kept running until I hit something and would have fallen to the ground if it wasn't for two hands grabbing me.

"I knew you'd fall for me," Alistair said with a chuckle. Then he stepped between me and Pandora. This time Alistair didn't have a broom, but he still had that same intimidating stare.

She flapped her wings a few times, even looking like she'd advance, but at the last minute she trotted off. Happy to pretend she wasn't scared of Alistair at all.

"Thanks for the rescue. Again." I dusted off my shorts even though I hadn't actually fallen. I was also sweating a lot, and I was lucky I hadn't stuck to Alistair.

"Or maybe that makes you unlucky," Detective Black said.

"Are you okay? Miles rang me to tell me you had asked for Kelly's address."

Clever Miles. "Sorry, I should have let you know myself, but I was excited about this lead, and I didn't think Kelly was dangerous. I still don't. Emblyn told me she saw Kelly and Sophia arguing. I didn't think they knew each other, but they do. Something is fishy there. She said she didn't want to tell me, but that she'd tell the police."

"Interesting."

"She clearly has a secret, but do you really think she could have killed her own family? Especially like that. There was so much blood." I shivered.

"If it was premeditated, then she would have known that. They have the same disease."

"Excuse me, say what now?"

"Right. Carl had Von Willebrand's disease. His GP let us know before the autopsy. I'm sorry I didn't tell you. He died of blunt force trauma as we suspected, and the disease isn't really important. It just explains why there was so much blood. Now, let's go see what Kelly has to say for herself."

I started following him as I Googled the disease. "Holy cowbell," I said and stopped. "I know who the killer is."

Chapter 22

It took us a while to locate Sophia, but she was hanging out at my bookshop, as it so happened, chatting with Eddie.

Alistair and I approached her.

"Sophia, can we talk a bit, it's important."

She eyed us warily and glanced at Eddie. Classic damsel-in-distress move.

"What's this about?" he asked.

"Now, please. Follow us," Alistair said.

"Okay, sure." She followed me as I made it through the door marked 'private.' I stopped and turned around. "You're Carl's daughter."

She glanced from me to Alistair, then nodded. "Yeah."

"And the reason you kept this from the police during a murder investigation is...?" Alistair asked.

"It was personal," she said. "I didn't want anybody to look at me differently or talk about Carl differently. I know he wasn't perfect."

"How come you don't have his name?" Alistair asked.

"Because he paid your mother to abort you, didn't he?" I said.

She looked away and closed her eyes for a second. "Yes. But she didn't. She raised me. She's a great mum."

"But you still wanted to find your father. He is your father, after all. Only you didn't want him to know, did you? That's why you coloured your hair."

She touched it. "Yes, well, the copper hair does stand out a bit. I didn't expect him to recognise my last name, I'm not sure he even knew my mum's surname. But still, it was disappointing when he didn't recognise me at all."

"But he knew. He knew when you started bleeding, because Von Willebrand's disease is hereditary. And he still didn't want anything to do with you. That's why he paid you off. And that's why you killed him," I said.

She gasped at this. "I swear I didn't kill him. I mean, I was disappointed. I was looking forward to working with him, learning from him, but again, I knew what he was like. I had expected it."

"You met him at the church, though. Didn't you?" Alistair asked.

"No, I was with Eddie. He said he'd wanted me to meet him at the church around midnight, but I decided not to go after I had such fun with Eddie. But Carl and I had fought before that. When he said he wanted to meet me, he also let me know that he knew. It was obvious he wasn't thrilled, and I figured he'd tell me to leave him alone, which I would have done. I have my pride."

She looked at Alistair. "Am I under arrest?"

"I want you to come to the station with me and make a formal statement."

She nodded.

"I'll tell Eddie," I said. Though not while he was in the shop.

Alistair gave me a nod. "I'll contact you later." They left through the back.

I sat down on the stairs and sighed. I was so sure that she'd killed him.

"What if she has?" Detective Black said. "Or, what if she's the one being set up now?"

"Not helping," I groaned.

Still, it didn't make sense that Carl got hold of Sophia's unfinished manuscript and then hid it in the Pembroke library, which meant that it had to be important.

I went up to my flat and grabbed my laptop, which was still on my bed. If I skimmed it, I could finish it quickly and maybe realise why it mattered.

I'd reached chapter seven when Eddie came into my bedroom.

"It's my break. What happened with Sophia?" he asked.

"Right. Sorry I didn't tell you, but the bookshop wasn't the place. Although, knowing Castlefield, people will find out soon enough."

"Find out what?" He sat down on the bed next to me.

"Sophia is Carl's daughter. I was sure she'd killed him, but she says she didn't. Alistair is interviewing her now."

"She's Carl's daughter? Are you serious? I would have never guessed that."

"Yes, she says she didn't want people to treat her differently after he died. And Carl didn't realise it until she had her bloody nose. They both have Von Willebrand's disease, and it's hereditary. It means that blood doesn't clot properly, and you bruise easily."

"Wow. So, she hadn't told Carl either?"

"Nope. And that's why I thought he had asked for the briefcase. To pay her off, get rid of her."

"But she couldn't have done it. She was with me, remember? We were both out like a light after that pizza."

I bit my lip. "And she couldn't have sneaked out?"

"You know I'm a light sleeper. Once, I woke up because someone burped outside. The window hadn't even been open."

I chuckled, then turned serious. "I feel like I've been running around in circles."

"It's not your problem. You're not a detective, and you don't have to solve this."

That's where he was wrong. I had to solve this. If I gave up, the killer would win. And that meant he could kill again. Instead of saying any of that, I just smiled.

After Eddie left, I continued reading. I wasn't sure if it would lead to anything, but I simply had to try.

"What's happening so far?" Detective Black asked.

"A woman becomes friends with a man that she clearly knows, but he doesn't recognise her. She wants to keep it that way. She then convinces the man to pretend to be murdered so she can solve the murder in the company of a detective and reveal they're smarter than he is. The detective is an old school friend of the man, and he's eager to show him up."

Detective Black didn't say anything. He paced around instead.

When I reached the part of the fake murder, I made myself a sandwich. I checked my watch. Would Alistair be hungry? Did he make his own lunch or would he go out and buy some in the village? Had Sophia been let go already?

I devoured my sandwich, then made a new one for Alistair. I took the bus to the police station and asked for him.

"He won't be a moment," a constable with braces said.

I waited by the counter until he showed, but he looked right past me. I followed his gaze. Kelly was there.

She looked pale and was sweating.

"Kelly, are you okay?" I asked.

She only had eyes for Alistair and ignored me completely. "I want to confess to the murder of Carl Scranton," she said.

ALISTAIR ARRESTED HER on the spot, and I was left behind, baffled. I was too curious to go home and carry on as if nothing had happened. I had invested so much time and energy that I needed to know. I sat down in the waiting area as my mind went through what could have happened. My thoughts were all tangled, and I ended up eating Alistair's sandwich. Accidentally.

"Why would she confess now?" asked Detective Black.

She'd seemed ready to share the reason for her argument with Sophia with the police. Perhaps she had been ready to come clean then, and we were simply sidetracked by Sophia's connection to Carl. Although it was an important sidetrack.

Did this mean that the fight was related to the murder? I couldn't help but wonder. Had Sophia been there? Had they done it together? Or did Sophia have nothing to do with the murder?

My mind went back to the manuscript. I promised myself I would wait an hour and then go back to read it all.

I waited a full two minutes before I left.

When I got to the flat, I continued reading and this time didn't stop until I was finished. The big twist in the story was that the man who was to pretend to get murdered actually got murdered. It stopped at the reveal of the killer's identity. It hadn't been written. At least, not in this version. At the park Sophia had said she was pretty much done. But even without the ending, I couldn't see why this had been important to Carl.

Just then someone came up the stairs. I left my bedroom to see who it was.

"Hey," Alistair said.

"Hey," I said.

A moment later we were in the kitchen where I'd made him a sandwich and a cool glass of lemonade.

"I've got to say that I'm glad this case is finally over," Alistair said and took a bite of his cheese sandwich.

"So, it really is her then? Kelly is the killer?" I asked.

"Yes, she met Carl at the church to give him a piece of her mind. Then he tried to bribe her to leave her alone, and she lost it."

"Why would he bribe her if he was using her to give him a place to stay?"

"She was kicking up a storm, apparently. They'd had a few fights because she'd been standing up to him. She was becoming a nuisance."

"But then why did she leave the murder weapon at the antique shop? And why with Wendy's hair? How had she even gotten it?"

"She freaked out afterwards and decided to blame it on someone else. She found the hair on his sleeve and put it there. Didn't even know who it belonged to."

"But why didn't she leave the hair on his body? Or leave the murder weapon behind?"

Alistair shrugged. "I don't know. She said she wasn't thinking straight."

Everything about this seemed to me as if the killer had been thinking straight. It was actually very calculated. But perhaps I was wrong.

"Hm."

Alistair grinned. "It really is over. She has an answer for everything. The reason she came forward now was because Sophia was questioned. She didn't want her to take the blame. She knew they were related. That's what the fight had been about. She had wanted Sophia to tell Carl the truth, but Sophia was worried he might reject her. She wanted to spend time with him, learn from him. Perhaps also make a profit by working together, I don't know."

"And after he died?" I asked.

"Sophia said that it made it less real if she just pretended not to be related. She also didn't want people to make a fuss."

"Eddie said he hadn't a clue, and he's been spending a lot of time with her. Don't you think it's odd that she showed no signs of grief at all?" I asked.

"She probably did, but in private. One thing you can never predict is how someone will grieve. It's very personal."

"Yes, I suppose it is. Thanks for coming to tell me."

"Hey, if I'd known you would feed me, I would have come sooner."

"I brought you a sandwich at the station, but then I got so anxious waiting that I ate it." I smiled apologetically.

He laughed. "Well, thanks for making it up to me."

"You're welcome."

"I guess this means I'm not your Watson anymore."

"No, I guess not." I smiled sadly.

"Regular friends it is then. And hopefully no more murders."

"Are you sure you want to wish that? You'd be out of a job."

"True, but in an ideal world I wouldn't have one. I'd simply resort to solving crimes in novels."

"I'd be happy to make them extra challenging for you then."

He smiled. "Thank you."

"SO THE CASE IS CLOSED," Eleanor said the next morning.

Last night the book club women, and the rest of the village, had heard the news. They also congratulated me, even though I'd assured them I had very little to do with the wrap-up.

"How do you feel about it?" Eleanor asked.

"I don't know. It doesn't sit right with me."

She laughed.

"What?"

"Are you sure you're not saying that because you don't want this case to be over?"

"Why would I not want this case to be over? I love mysteries, but not that much."

She gave me a knowing smile. "But you do love spending time with Alistair."

I bit my lip. "I mean, I do, but that wouldn't be a reason to want to look into a murder investigation any longer than necessary."

"If you say so," she said with a giggle.

Was she right? Was that really the reason?

"Don't doubt yourself," Detective Black said. "You should trust your instincts more."

"Did you know that Alistair is the opening act for the talent show this afternoon?" Eleanor said.

"He is? Is he doing magic tricks?"

"Yes," she exclaimed. "How did you know that?"

"Well, it's either that or knitting," I said.

"He knits as well? My, he really is a man of many talents, isn't he?"

"Yep."

"And handsome."

"Yep."

"And why are you not together again?" she asked.

"It's complicated."

"Dear girl, in my experience, love is never complicated. People are."

Chapter 23

Christina bought me a smoothie as we took a walk through the square. The market was yet again in full swing. We ended up at the standing tables near the vicarage where we enjoyed a few snacks and bought lemonade from a stand monitored by two kids wearing oversized straw hats.

We talked about how one of the tourists had mistaken Pandora for a normal chicken and had tried feeding her, but we inevitably ended up discussing Carl's murder.

"I'm just not sure if it fits, but I could be wrong," I said.

"What is the piece of the puzzle that's missing?" Christina asked.

I told her about the manuscript that Carl had hidden in the library.

"Is there any way for you to reach her laptop?"

My eyes widened. "Christina, are you suggesting I sneak into her room in the B&B and snoop around on her laptop?"

"Well, for instance."

That would be doable, I realised.

"I'll help," she said.

"It sounds more exciting than it will be, probably."

"That's okay. I could distract Mrs Suzuki while you go up."

The door lock could be picked, but her laptop would probably be password protected. Still, I could try.

"Do you know where Sophia is?"

Christina nodded. "She is right over there."

I looked up. She, together with the Castlefield Book Club, was helping to set up the stage for the talent show. It was a very simple stage and each year the book club helped set it up because they always performed. There were occasionally one or two new people that tried something, but most years it stayed the same.

Phoebe and Jessica would do a tap dancing routine. They were surprisingly good, even if their outfits were made of awful colours that made you wish you were colour blind.

Nancy, Olivia, and Eleanor would sing, and Ava, Lily, and Poppy would do something different each year. Last year it was building an elaborate house of cards, the year before that it was fruit carving.

"Okay, let's try and see what we can find out," I said, not sure if we would yield results but relieved I wasn't giving up just yet.

MRS SUZUKI OPENED THE door wearing large sunglasses. She smiled. "I was just on my way out. Do you need anything?"

"Actually," I said, glancing at Christina who was giving her best smile. "I want to leave something for Sophia. It's a present. Don't tell her, it's a surprise."

"Oh, that's kind of you. I was shocked to learn that she's that murdered man's daughter. Poor girl. I'll be heading out, so make sure you close the door firmly behind you. All the guests are out. She's in the first room on the right." She gave a wave and trotted off.

"This is excellent," Christina whispered.

"I know." We went inside and shut the door. "I was afraid she'd ask me about the present."

"I'm glad she didn't." Christina gave a nervous giggle. "This is so exciting."

I smiled and went up the stairs first. When we reached Sophia's room, I took out my lock pick set and started fumbling with the lock.

Christina looked around furtively, even though there was nobody who could interrupt us. "I'm so relieved you know about all this stuff. I wouldn't know where to begin. Also, I'd probably panic and end up breaking stuff."

"Don't worry, we're together, and we can always lie. When I was seventeen I had a holiday fling with a boy, and I thought he was cheating on me so when he said he'd go swimming with mates, I followed him to a house and tried to peer over the bushes. There was an annoying dog that started harassing me, and I ended up *in* the bushes. He found me. It was utterly embarrassing, so I told him I had been walking down the street to visit Eleanor and had been chased by a dog. He believed it. And no, he was not cheating on me."

Christina laughed. "I'm sorry, but that's funny. And good thinking."

The door opened when I pulled on the handle. "Voila, my lady," I said as the door swung open.

She applauded. "Now what?"

"We go in."

She looked at me as if I'd just suggested eating a wooden bowl. "What?"

"Nothing," she said. "I know this was my suggestion, but it just feels weird to trespass. Like we're intruding."

"We kind of are, but if she's a murderer then it will be worth it." I stepped into the room.

"What if she's not?"

"Then we buy her a gift basket." I spotted her laptop on the bed. "Bingo."

Christina finally followed me inside and shut the door behind her. She remained near it, as if it would make the intrusion less severe. I, on the other hand, was already next to the bed and had her laptop open. There was very little in the room. She had one purple suitcase which was half open and had mostly clothes in it. Other than that, there were a hairbrush and a phone charger on the nightstand.

The laptop was password protected, and I tried a few things. There was pretty much no chance of me guessing the password, but I had to try. I'd already decided that if this didn't work, I would simply ask her to let me read the ending. If she was really innocent, she would let me.

I tried several passwords, including the name of her main character from her new book as well as the new manuscript. There was a chance it would work since Detective Black was my password for most things. Except that it didn't work.

"She came into the bookshop to buy a book from her favourite author," Christina said, now moving closer to the bed.

"Really? Who?"

"Agatha Christie."

I tried that and gasped. "We're in."

"No way!" Christina sat down next to me. My heart was racing and my palms sweaty. "Okay, calm down. Let's check out her documents." I scoured for a map labelled 'writing' or even 'work,' but couldn't find it. She had a lot of open tabs on book blogs, and it was clear that she liked reading, but where were her manuscripts? I even checked the latest documents but they were nothing of interest to me.

"That's weird. What kind of writer doesn't have her novels on her laptop?"

Christina frowned. "That is strange. She was working on it, you said."

"Yep, but I only have her word for it. I never actually saw the screen. I don't get it. The manuscript that Carl had hidden had her name on it. But...it's almost as if she's not written it. Or, she simply has two laptops. That's the only explanation."

"Then we should ask her that. In a non-obvious way. Somehow. Like: 'I have two similar dresses, isn't that funny? Do you have two laptops?'"

I laughed. "Yes, that sounds completely normal."

"What? It's just a suggestion."

"I will ask her, but I'll work it into the conversation a bit more naturally than that," I said.

Christina stuck her tongue out.

We left everything as we'd found it and went back to the square. There was a breeze that made it feel cooler, and it was the first time since a long time that walking so much as ten feet didn't cause me to sweat like crazy.

"There she is," Christina said, as we reached the square.

She was standing there chatting with Nancy and Gus. It was nice to see them together. They looked like a proper couple. Just as Nancy and Gus walked off to Nancy's shop, we reached Sophia.

"Hey, want to have a drink at the pub with us?" Christina said, before I could. "You've been working hard on the stage."

It did look really professional. The chairs for the audience had also been set up.

"I'd love to. I'm dying from thirst," she said. "Pardon my word choice."

THE PUB WAS NICE AND cool, and we all ordered non-alcoholic drinks. Christina was a star. She managed to chat Sophia's ear off about fashion, books, even Snowball.

Sophia either really enjoyed those topics, or she was very good at pretending to be interested.

When the topic landed on offices and writing, it was my cue. "It's really important to be organised for me," I said. "That's why I had two laptops for a while. One specifically for my writing. Is that weird?"

"No, not at all. My mum...my mum did that too."

"Your mum writes too?" Christina chirped. "That's so cool. Is she published?"

Sophia blushed and shook her head.

I cleared my throat. "But do you do that too? Or do you not need to stay organised that way?"

"No, I just have the one laptop, it's easier that way." She smiled.

"Yes, I suppose that's why I went back to one laptop as well," I said, and followed up with a few more writing questions so that hopefully this very important question didn't stick out. But while Sophia was politely engaging in the conversation, my mind reeled.

If she had only one laptop, then where the hell were her manuscripts? The only thing I could think of was that Carl had maybe stolen all of her manuscripts and deleted them from her laptop, like he had with Rachel. Which meant that maybe, if she had indeed killed him, she had them somewhere on a USB stick. Too many what-ifs, still.

What was I missing?

AFTER OUR DRINKS, SOPHIA left to hang out with Wendy and Gregor. She said they had to arrange their way back to Devon, something they hadn't done yet with all that had been going on with Carl.

"When will you leave?" I asked.

"Tomorrow, probably."

Christina and I looked at each other.

"Eddie will be sad," I said.

"I know. He's very sweet." She smiled, but didn't say any more than that.

"Could I have your number? I'd like to stay in touch." I took out my phone.

"Sure." She typed it into my phone, and I saved it.

"Thanks, see you around," I said.

"Bye." She left.

Christina and I turned to each other.

"So, what does this mean?" Christina asked.

"Do you think that Carl stole her manuscripts? And she confronted him?"

Christina shrugged. "I really don't know. Anything is possible."

"Right," I said.

Detective Black sat opposite of me. "I still think the manuscript is important," he said.

I felt that too, but where to dig deeper? Did the answers lie with Sophia? Wendy? Gregor? Rachel? Kelly?

NOTHING COULD MAKE me feel as peaceful as a visit to Beth, so that's where I headed after our drinks while Christina went back to the Wicked Bookworm.

Beth gave me a raspberry tart that she'd made with Eleanor in the morning, and I savoured every bite as we sat in the garden again.

"Alistair came round yesterday," Beth said.

"He did?" I said with my mouth full.

She nodded. "Handsome young man. He showed me these magic tricks for this afternoon. It was so impressive. My hands were sore from clapping."

The idea of him performing magic tricks and impressing Beth made me melt, and not because of the heat. "That is wonderful," I said.

"I told him he could do with an assistant and that Poppy would really like that, and he said he'd ask her. I wonder if he did."

"But isn't she going to perform with—no, wait, I suppose she could do both. Can't she?"

"Yes, I'm sure it's not a problem. A few years ago I performed twice. I played the keyboard, and I did a mime act. Not a lot of people joined that year, so they were happy to let me do two acts."

"Y—you mimed?" I bit my lip to keep from laughing.

"Yes. I painted my whole face white, and I had one of those striped shirts on. I looked quite fetching."

"I don't remember that."

"Ah, it was a while back. It was a year when lots of people went on holiday."

"Maybe it was when Nancy took me through the south of England in that camper."

"It could be," she said. "Did you know that Alistair is terribly afraid of frogs?"

"Is he?" Why did that make me like him more?

"Mark was afraid of butterflies. Didn't make any sense to me, but me being terrified of spiders didn't make sense to him." She smiled.

"Do you still miss him a lot?" I asked.

"Oh, yes. I mean, we argued like any couple and sometimes drove each other mad, I tell you, but he was the love of my life. Sometimes I'll see or hear something that I know would have made him laugh, and I look at the spot where he would always sit to see his reaction. But of course, he's not there."

I touched her arm.

"But we had a good life together, we made such nice memories. That's really what it's all about, making nice memories. Experiencing things that make you happy. And one day I'll be with him again, and all I would have to say is: thank you and I love you."

I tried my best not to cry.

"We met at a party, and his friend was flirting with me. Then another guy bumped into me and spilled his drink all over my new dress. I had saved up months for that dress, I remember. The friend just laughed and then Mark, who had been on my other side, he just punched his friend."

"Wow."

"Yes. Afterwards Mark told me he had no idea what had come over him. Just that he felt the need to protect me. I guess he's always felt that need. Just like I've always wanted to protect him."

I really, really wanted a relationship like that.

After we chatted for a bit longer, I helped her water the plants in the garden and went on my way. The talent show would start in half an hour. Just as I was on my way over, I passed the vicarage and Harold wheeled over. "Maggie, sorry to have to ask, but could you help out in the cellar? We need to get the wine up in the church for tomorrow's wine tasting, but Eleanor has been invited to have a drink with the girls after the talent show. Would you mind helping? There's still about four crates left, but you don't have to do them all, or at all, I mean, if you're busy."

I knew he meant it. He was not the sort to manipulate or guilt trip anyone, which is exactly why I wanted to help. I still had thirty minutes.

"Sure," I said.

"Thank you. Thank you so much. You know how to access the cellar, right? Door in the far right corner. I'll go ask for some more hands, I can't let you do it all alone." He was off before I could respond.

I headed around to the entrance of the church and stepped into the cool church. The benches had been moved and tables had been set up for the tasting tomorrow. Crates with wine were scattered throughout the room. The door in the back was already open. It was an old wooden door and stone steps coiled down to the dark and musty cellar. There was a lightbulb in the middle that provided some light, and the cellar itself was capacious and tidy with several pillars spread evenly throughout the space. The crate of wine was quite heavy, and it took me a lot of effort and sweat to get it up to the church. I returned for a second crate and was rummaging around, trying to get a good handle on it, when someone's footfalls sounded behind me. I put the crate back down and turned around.

Something hard hit my face, pain spreading through my skull like a wave of needles, and I fell to the floor.

Chapter 24

Something warm trickled over my forehead, and I groaned. There was a moment of silence when someone moved away from me and then closer.

My head was pounding and my vision blurry for a moment. I blinked rapidly.

"Why?" I groaned, as my hands were tied behind my back. Something scraped over the floor and Sophia came into view as she pulled me into a sitting position.

"I'm sorry, I just—I can't kill you," she said. Her hands were shaking. The crowbar with which she'd hit me was on the ground next to me. She picked me up with difficulty, and we both fell to the ground a few times. She eventually put me in the chair and tied my ankles to the legs of the chair.

Then she started pacing up and down and groaned herself. "I—I just need to stay calm. Don't make a sound," she said to me. "I'll be back." She ran off.

My head was pounding too hard for me to think of something brilliant to say, so instead I shouted: "Don't forget the milk."

"Don't lose it now," Detective Black said as he frowned at me.

"I haven't lost it, I've still got it. What are we talking about?"

"You need to focus. You have the knife."

"I just want a lot of aspirin and a nap."

"No, no," he said. "Don't fall asleep. You need to get out of here."

"What is it with murderers and hitting me on the head?"

"I'm not sure if she's a murderer."

It hurt to think back even just a few seconds. "You're right. She was panicked." I leaned forward and then back, trying to reach into the back of my shorts for my knife. It wasn't easy to get my fingers around it and grip it tightly enough not to risk dropping it as I pulled it out. Blood trickled over my face.

After slow agonising movements, I finally had the knife in my palm. I cut myself trying to open it, but it worked. I tried to look behind me to see the rope, but I couldn't. Instead I felt around, picked a part, and started moving the knife up and down.

I closed my eyes and pretended I was in the flat, practising this while Christina was timing me. Oh, great. Time. I had to hurry, or Sophia would be back. And she wouldn't be alone.

Detective Black encouraged me while I kept at it. My wrists felt like they were on fire, but I couldn't stop. I nearly cried when my wrists moved apart.

"Good, now hurry up and do your ankles," Detective Black said.

I was about to when I heard a noise and footsteps. I folded the knife and tucked it in the back of my trousers. With my hands pressed together it would look like I was still tied up. I also leaned forward slightly, as if I was dazed by the hit.

Sophia first came in view. The second woman was Rachel.

"I knew it was only a matter of time with you snooping around," Rachel said. "You are like a dog with a bone. I rather liked it. It felt like a game. You're an interesting adversary." She smiled, but there was no warmth. Nothing about what she'd shown to me was real. There was a cool killer behind her friendly face.

I blinked and groaned as my headache was getting worse. "You're the one who wrote the manuscript. You were setting him up from the beginning. You set everything up from the beginning. The manuscript is the story of how you killed him. I mean, it wasn't exactly the same. He was a professional golfer, killed with his golf club, but Carl was an author and he was killed with his award."

"Ha! He was a thief, not an author. And he deserved to die. He hadn't changed one bit," Rachel said.

Sophia was standing behind her and had scrunched up her face as if she was about to cry any moment. But them standing together...I saw it.

"You're Sophia's mother. Carl got you pregnant."

Rachel rolled her eyes. "Duh. I remarried and Sophia took his last name. Carl didn't even come close to recognising her, the fool."

"Until she bled, and he realised she was his daughter. Not that he guessed who the mother was, I reckon. Or did he?" I said.

"Nope. He just thought I was part of the plan to fake his murder. He thought Sophia had hired me or something. He probably believed I still had no clue that he had stolen my manuscript."

"And how long had you planned this? I'm guessing Sophia's first book is also really yours, isn't it?"

"Oh, yes. I know I'm good. Carl's first book was a bestseller, and that was a book I wrote. I mean, I know I accused him when he was reading his latest book, but it was actually his first novel which was originally mine. It didn't take me long to get Sophia published. And it didn't take me long to put her on his radar. I wrote *Poised to Quill* just for him. Sophia convinced him to pretend to get killed, said that the pathologist would be in on it, that they could make people think that he was dead. He'd read about you and that you had solved an earlier case. He wanted to do that. He wanted to show you and the police up, make the newspapers. He loved the idea of fooling people, of showing up dramatically to announce he hadn't been killed."

"But in order to do that, Sophia had to convince him to work with her on the manuscript. And he either got curious, or he was planning on stealing it anyway, but he got a hold of it."

"I was at least smart enough to put her name on the manuscript, but yes, he got a hold of it. It was on a flash drive that he'd stolen. And he must have realised that Sophia's real plan was to kill him, after he saw her nosebleed." Rachel laughed. "It was so fun to watch him squirm. He wanted to keep the novel, and he wanted to pay her off. Get rid of her. Just like he had twenty years ago when I told him I was pregnant. The bastard. As if we would touch his money. And Kelly fell for Sophia's confession and wanted to protect her. Dumb woman."

Sophia started biting her nails.

"Wait. Sophia was at the church that night?"

Sophia looked at the ground while Rachel laughed again. It was a sound that made my bones shiver. "Yes, poor Eddie. She gave him Wendy's sleeping pills. He was out like a light."

I nearly jumped up and hit her. "You bitch. Both of you are evil!"

"Yes, yes. Save it for—well, never. You're going to die. That's a fact. I win. You lose." She clapped her hands. "Get those crates up," she told Sophia. "I don't want anyone to have a reason to come down here."

Sophia glanced at me, but then did as she was told.

Rachel turned back to me. "If you don't mind, I'm going to get a bit creative with your murder. I'll be right back." She disappeared up the stairs while Sophia carried one of the crates.

"Please, Sophia, don't do this. I can't die yet. There's still so much cheesecake to eat, and I think I want children, even though it terrifies me, and I'm really excited about this next book I'm working on, as well as I'm pretty infatuated with someone, and I haven't properly enjoyed it yet. Please, don't do this. You have the power to stop it."

Sophia kept on walking and reached the stairs. She ignored my pleas and soon was out of sight.

I grabbed my knife and started working on my left leg, but I hadn't gotten through the rope yet before Sophia returned for the next crate. I pleaded again, until she was out of sight, then went back to the rope. When I cut through it, I threw the rope in a dark corner, then worked on the next one. Sophia didn't notice when she returned. And so it went on, until I had freed both my legs, but this time, before I could do anything, they both returned.

I sat there, as innocently as possible, the only difference being that the rope around my ankles was gone, and I prayed that they wouldn't notice.

"I've always wanted to do this," Rachel said and she tied a rope around my chest, the knot right under my breasts. The other end of the rope, she tied around one of the pillars, tilting me back on the two back legs of the chair. I was so afraid to move, I was holding my breath. Only the rope kept me from falling back.

Below me she placed a sharp rake, it was right where my head would be if I fell backwards, which she took the time to explain to me.

Lovely.

Pure pride kept me from crying. She then moved the table near the rope and placed a candle under it. "It's only a matter of time before you die, but we will make sure we have alibis. It will be difficult for the police to prove it was us."

"Yeah, no, great. Looks like you've got it all figured out," I said.

Rachel grinned. "I like you, Maggie."

"Great, wonderful. Let's go and get some tea, have a chat. Be friends."

She lit the candle and nodded at Sophia. "Let's get ourselves an alibi."

Sophia followed her mother, but glanced back. Her eyes went to my ankles, but she didn't say anything.

The moment they were gone I cried. With trembling hands I slowly reached up to the rope and then pulled. When all four legs touched the floor I worked on the rope around my chest. As soon as that was off, I let myself fall to the floor and sobbed uncontrollably for about a minute before I managed to pull myself together. I would cry more later, but for now I had to make sure they didn't get away with the murder of Carl Scranton, nor my attempted murder.

The flame had touched the rope by now and I stomped out the part that had started to burn. I also blew out the candle and though my legs were shaking, I made it upstairs. My head was still pounding, and I felt dizzy.

The door was locked. Or blocked, I couldn't tell.

"Your phone," Detective Black said.

"Right, of course." I fished it out of my pocket and dialled Alistair. It took me a while because I was shaking. The bright light of my screen in the poorly lit staircase didn't help my headache at all.

The phone rang. And rang. He would probably be on stage. And most people would be there. The best way to confront them would be in a crowd. It was my only chance, but only if I got out of here. I texted Alistair that Rachel and Sophia were responsible for Carl's murder and that they'd tried to kill me and hoped he would secretly check it during his performance, though it was unlikely.

"Help!" I started shouting as I banged on the door.

"Call Harold," Detective Black said. "He always picks up the phone, and he never has it on silent."

There was a noise on the other side and the door swung open suddenly. I was so worried that it was Rachel and Sophia, that they had still been there, that I took a step back.

Christina opened the door, and I fell into her arms, crying.

"Maggie," she said. "I'm so glad you're okay."

"How did you know I was in trouble?" I sobbed, barely coherent.

"Eddie said that Harold needed help in the cellar, but when I walked up to the vicarage I ran into Rachel and Sophia. It was odd to see them together, and they were so adamant that everything was all settled here that I knew something was up. I pretended to be on my way home, but returned. You're bleeding," she said as she pulled back to observe my face.

"I will tell you later, but for now we have to stop them. They'll be at the talent show. After that I'll go to the doctor, I promise."

"Let's go."

Christina supported me as we walked down to the village square, taking a slight detour since the vicarage looked out over the square, and we didn't want them to see us coming. We hurried along. Luckily, we didn't gather the attention of anyone except Pandora. She observed me, then started walking alongside us. It was as if she was on the same warpath as we were after observing my injuries.

We made it to the back of the audience. There was an aisle in the middle of the chairs. Alistair was on the stage. He was dressed in black and had on a purple cape with glitters. He looked every part the magician. Poppy was next to him. She was brave considering the fact that she was 83 years old and dressed in what can only be described as a bathing suit with glitter. She was making arm movements as Alistair did a card trick. His eyes scanned the crowd as everyone applauded when his eyes landed on me. His smile faltered.

I mouthed Rachel's name and drew Rachel's initial in the air, mirrored so he could see it clearly. Hopefully. She was the actual murderer, after all. Sophia would let herself get caught, Rachel was more dangerous.

"Okay, for my next trick, I need a volunteer," Alistair said. "You there." He pointed at someone in the crowd. I couldn't make out who from all the way in the back, but Rachel was the one who got up. People applauded.

Oh, if only they knew what a psycho she was.

She made her way to the stage, focussed on Alistair. This was good, since it meant she hadn't seen me yet.

"Wonderful," Alistair said, then looked at me.

I nodded.

He took his handcuffs out and put them on her wrists. "You're under arrest for the murder of Carl Scranton, as well as for the attempted murder on Maggie Matthews." He looked back at me. Now the rest of the crowd turned back to look at me. I shouldn't have worn so much blood today.

"She what?!" Nancy shouted. "What did you just say?" She came up from the front row in a sparkly purple dress, which she was wearing for her performance.

Christina and I made our way to the front. "Before Nancy starts beating up Rachel, Sophia was also involved with the murder. And she's the one that actually hit me," I said.

Nancy let out a primal cry and Sophia got up to run. She'd only taken a few steps before Eddie had tackled her.

Pandora then joined in by picking at her ankles, while Nancy started hitting Sophia with a broom.

"Where did she get that broom from?" Christina asked.

"Don't even ask," I muttered.

Chapter 25

Wednesday night was the last night of the Summer Festival. This would be my favourite day since this was the dance. The entire square looked like a fairy tale with lights in trees as well as across the square itself, from shop to shop. There were no chairs, just a lot of blankets and cushions on the ground so you could sit or even lie down.

There was a band performing, and the music would be gentle. The kind of music where you would gladly dance in someone's arms all night.

Christina and I were getting ready at the flat. She had done my makeup and was now doing up my red dress. "And then Poppy tackled Rachel straight off the podium like she was in an action film."

"I know. She does that sometimes. At least both Rachel and Sophia learned that you don't mess with the Castlefield villagers."

"You've got that right." Her smile vanished and she looked down. "But poor Eddie. He was really upset."

"I know. I think it helped when we had that movie marathon here. He seemed a bit more like himself. But still, it will probably take him a while to get over it. You don't find out every day that the girl you fancy drugged you so her mother could kill her father."

"What about you?" She brushed the hairs out of my face to reveal the stitches I had needed.

"I might require a few therapy sessions, but I'm just happy that it all worked out in the end. Thanks for coming to my rescue." I hugged her.

"Anytime," she said. "And listen, there's something else I have to say."

"What?"

"You know how Alistair's been fussing over you these past few days?"

I shook my head as I went through the mental list. "He's brought two fruit baskets, a teddy bear, chocolate, and a foot massager."

"Yes, but he did that because he loves you. And I'll admit that it was weird when I realised he had a thing for you, but it's okay now. I want you both to be happy. Maybe I want you to be happy a bit more than I want him to be happy, but still." She laughed. "You have my blessing. Go for it."

I blinked away tears.

"Aww, no don't cry. It's fine. No more crying. Let's be happy." She tapped my nose. "Come on, we've got empty dance cards that need to be filled."

The square was like a fairy tale, and Christina's eyes almost fell out as she admired it. "This is amazing. I want the village square to always look like this."

"Me too."

The entire square was full, but the space in front of the band was kept empty for people to dance. After we had found Eddie and Nancy, Harold tapped the microphone.

"We may have had a few difficult days in Castlefield, but we are a family, and we can get through anything. Especially when Maggie Matthews is our champion sleuth." The crowd applauded and Alistair, who was closer to the band, whistled.

I felt my cheeks get red. This time it was nice to be praised, though. But that was probably because I'd come close to dying. Again.

"I hereby declare the Summer Festival dance of 2020 opened," Harold shouted, and while the crowd erupted in applause, the band started playing. Couples immediately took to the dance floor.

I danced with every single woman of the book club, with Beth, Emblyn, Eddie, Gus, Harold, and eventually with Alistair.

He took me in his arms like he had that time at his place, and it felt just as wonderful. Nancy was dancing with Gus, who winked at me as they whirled past us. Though this was a slow song, their dance was not.

"How are you feeling?"

"You've already asked me that three times today. In fact, I had to silence my phone."

He laughed. "Well, sorry for caring."

"No, that part is definitely fine. It's just that you don't have to worry. I really am fine."

"Your whole neck and shoulder were covered in blood. It really was awful to see. I don't ever want to see any blood on you ever again," he said in a stern tone.

"Really? And just when I heard it is becoming a trend this autumn. I don't want to fall behind on the latest fashion trends. I have a reputation to uphold."

"That's not funny."

"I beg to differ. Besides, I hadn't planned on it. I was just minding my own business down there."

"I know it's not your fault. It's mine. I shouldn't have asked you to help me investigate. It was stupid. I just—I just wanted to be—I mean, I like spending time with you."

"It's alright. If you hadn't asked me, I still wouldn't have left it alone. We both know that. So please don't feel guilty. Let's be happy." I smiled at Christina's words, then thought about the other thing I had to tell Alistair.

"Listen, I really like you," I said.

"I like you too."

"But I really think we should remain friends. I mean, no more dancing or anything else that could be considered romantic."

He pressed his lips together. "Why?"

"Because Christina gave me her blessing, and it means that she's an amazing friend. I don't want to dive right into something with her ex. Especially when that ex is still figuring some stuff out."

Detective Black popped up next to us. "So? That's part of life. Don't waste any more time and jump his bones."

I did my best to ignore him.

Alistair smiled. "Yes, well, I wasn't planning on diving into anything. I just—like I said, I like being with you. So, friends, no romance."

"Yes, deal."

"May I cut in?" a familiar voice said.

We both looked up at Miles.

"Sure, why not?" I said.

Alistair kissed my hand as he maintained eye contact. A final moment of romance, and I savoured it. Then he left and Miles took his place.

"Did you make any romantic plans?" He wiggled his eyebrows.

"No, quite the opposite."

Miles made a face.

"What?"

"Nothing. It's just too bad. You'd make a cute couple."

"Thanks, but that's hardly a reason to date someone. We make a cute couple, for that matter."

He grinned. "Do you think so, darling? Well, I'm game if you are."

"In your dreams."

"Sure, there too."

I laughed.

"Have you thought of your reward yet? You still deserve one from helping me out."

"Oh, yes. I've thought about it," I said.

"And?"

"I want three get-out-of-jail-free cards. Not related to your lawyer skills necessarily, but I want to be able to call on you three times with you dropping everything and helping me with whatever I need. One of those occasions will probably be you cooking for me when I don't feel like doing it myself."

"As you wish," he said with a smile. "But knowing your propensity for trouble, you might want to save that one as well."

By the end of the night, my stomach was sore from laughter, my head woozy from the alcohol, and my happiness meter was full. At my request, Harold gave me the number of the guy he wanted to set me up with, and I had at least that to look forward to. And of course, the wrap-up of my latest novel.

DETECTIVE BLACK LOOKED out of the window and contemplated the past events. He had almost died at the hands of a killer. He had solved his latest case. He had made new friends.

As he looked at the people sitting across from him in the pub, he realised how lucky he was. Because he couldn't help but sometimes wonder what the bloody point was. Sometimes he would feel lonely in a crowd, feel lost when all was technically right. And then someone came to remind him what really mattered. He had nearly died, but it made him realise who he was and what he cared about. He wasn't alone. He was strong. And more importantly, he was happy.

The end.

Did you love *Poised to Quill*? Then you should read *The Exciting Life of a Minor Character*[1] by Morgan W. Silver!

[2]

Claire is sick of being a Minor Character. She despises the fact that the most exciting thing that's happened to her in four long years has been answering a phone.

She wants her own story, she wants more lines, and most of all, she wants adventure. Even if that means killing her Main Character. Unfortunately, only the Author has the power to kill Characters, but Claire will not be deterred by logic and facts.

---

1. https://books2read.com/u/mKDAXE

2. https://books2read.com/u/mKDAXE

Then, even though it's not supposed to be possible, someone is murdered in Character Central. It causes a widespread panic worse than the time they had a lemon shortage. After all, only the Author should have the ability to kill a Character.

With the threat of multiple victims as well as Erasure for all Characters, Claire must team up with the Main Character she wants to bring down. If all else fails, she may even have to take it up with the Author.

Read more at www.authormw.com.

Made in the USA
Las Vegas, NV
10 February 2024